I

THE EPIC OF GILGAMESH

II

ODYSSEUS RETURNS HOME HOMER

III

XERXES INVADES GREECE HERODOTUS

IV

'THE SEA, THE SEA' XENOPHON

V

THE ABDUCTION OF SITA

VI

JASON AND THE GOLDEN FLEECE APOLLONIUS

VII

EXODUS

VIII

THE DESTRUCTION OF TROY VIRGIL

IX

THE SERPENT'S TEETH OVID

X

THE FALL OF JERUSALEM JOSEPHUS

XI

THE MADNESS OF NERO TACITUS

XII

CUPID AND PSYCHE APULEIUS

XIII

THE LEGENDARY ADVENTURES OF ALEXANDER THE GREAT

XIV

BEOWULF

XV

SIEGFRIED'S MURDER

XVI

SAGAS AND MYTHS OF THE NORTHMEN

XVII

THE SUNJATA STORY

XVIII

THE DESCENT INTO HELL DANTE

XIX

KING ARTHUR'S LAST BATTLE MALORY

XX

THE VOYAGES OF SINDBAD

Apollonius of Rhodes

Jason and the Golden Fleece

TRANSLATED BY E. V. RIEU

PENGUIN EPICS

PENGUIN BOOKS

Published by the Penguin Group
Penguin Books Ltd, 80 Strand, London WC2R ORL, England
Penguin Group (USA) Inc., 375 Hudson Street, New York, New York 10014, USA
Penguin Group (Canada), 90 Eglinton Avenue East, Suite 700, Toronto, Ontario, Canada M4P 2Y3
(a division of Pearson Penguin Canada Inc.)
Penguin Ireland, 25 St Stephen's Green, Dublin 2, Ireland (a division of Penguin Books Ltd)
Penguin Group (Australia), 250 Camberwell Road, Camberwell, Victoria 3124, Australia
(a division of Pearson Australia Group Pty Ltd)
Penguin Books India Pvt Ltd, 11 Community Centre, Panchsheel Park, New Delhi – 110 017, India
Penguin Group (NZ), cnr Airborne and Rosedale Roads, Albany,
Auckland 1310, New Zealand (a division of Pearson New Zealand Ltd)
Penguin Books (South Africa) (Pty) Ltd, 24 Sturdee Avenue,
Rosebank, Johannesburg 2196, South Africa

Penguin Books Ltd, Registered Offices: 80 Strand, London WC2R ORL, England

www.penguin.com

This translation of *The Voyage of Argo* first published 1959
Second edition 1971
This extract published in Penguin Books 2006
3

Translation copyright © E. V. Rieu, 1959, 1971
All rights reserved

The moral right of the translator has been asserted

Taken from the Penguin Classics edition of *The Voyage of Argo*, translated by E. V. Rieu

Typeset by Rowland Phototypesetting Ltd, Bury St Edmunds, Suffolk
Printed in England by Clays Ltd, St Ives plc

ISBN-13: 978–0–141–02632–9
ISBN-10: 0–141–02632–4

Note

Jason and the Golden Fleece is taken from *The Voyage of Argo*, which was written by Apollonius of Rhodes in the third century BC. A story of high romance and incredible adventure, it tells of Jason's voyage in quest of the Golden Fleece. Here, the story begins with the journey underway, and the arrival of the Argonauts at the kingdom of Amycus, the king of the Bebryces.

This was where Amycus, the arrogant king of the Bebryces, had his farm and cattle-yards. Borne to Poseidon by the Bithynian nymph Melie, he was the world's greatest bully. It was his barbarous custom to allow no one, not even a foreign visitor, to leave his country before trying conclusions with him in a boxing-match. He had already killed a number of his neighbours. And now he came down to the ship, planted himself among the Argonauts and not even troubling to ask who they were or what had brought them overseas, had the effrontery to say:

'Listen, sailormen, to something you should know. No foreigner calling here is allowed to continue his journey without putting up his fists to mine. So pick out your best man and match him against me on the spot. Otherwise you will find to your sorrow that if you defy my laws you will be brought by main force to obey them.'

His high-handed manner roused them to fury, and Polydeuces, who took his threat as a personal affront, stepped forward at once to champion his friends.

'Enough!' he said. 'Whoever you may be, let us have no more of this parade of violence. You have stated your rules and we accept them. Here I am, ready to meet you of my own free will.'

He spoke bluntly, and Amycus glared at him with

rolling eyes, like a lion who is hit by a javelin when they hunt him in the mountains, and caring nothing for the crowd that hems him in, picks out the man who wounded him, and keeps his eyes on him alone.

Polydeuces was wearing a light and closely woven cloak, the parting gift of some Lemnian girl. This he now laid aside. The other threw down his dark double mantle with its clasps, and the knotty staff of mountain olive that he carried. Then they looked round, chose a satisfactory spot near by, and told their friends to sit down in separate groups on the sands.

In build and stature the two men showed a complete contrast. Amycus made one think of some monstrous offspring of the ogre Typhoeus or of Earth herself, the kind she used to bear in the old days of her quarrel with Zeus. But Polydeuces was like a star of heaven shining in all its beauty out of the western night. Such was the son of Zeus, with the bloom of the first down still on his cheeks and the twinkle still in his eyes, though in strength and spirit he was hardening like a wild beast.

He began by feinting with his arms to see whether they were still supple and not benumbed by all the hard work and rowing he had done. Amycus did not follow his example, but stood off in silence, eyeing his opponent and all agog at the thought of drawing blood from his breast. And now Amycus' steward Lycoreus placed between them, at the feet of each, a pair of raw-hide gloves thoroughly dried and toughened, and the king addressed the other in his domineering style:

'We will cast no lots for these, but to avoid recriminations later, I make you a present of whichever pair you fancy. So bind them on your hands. And when you have found out you can tell your friends how good I am at cutting dried ox-hide and staining a man's cheeks with blood.'

Polydeuces indulged in no answering taunt. With a quiet smile and no parley he took the pair that lay at his feet. Castor and the great Talaus came up and quickly bound his gauntlets on, with a flow of encouraging words, while Aretus and Ornytus did the same for their king, little knowing that, as ill luck decreed, it was for the last time.

They stood apart while this was being done, but when all was ready they put up their heavy fists in front of their faces and went for each other with a will. In a rough sea a great wave will curl up over a ship, but just as it seems ready to pour in across the bulwarks the steersman's skill saves her by a hair's breadth and away she slips. In much the same way, though the king attacked, always following up and never giving him a moment's rest, Polydeuces had the craft to avoid his rushes and remain unscathed. But there were weak points as well as strong in his opponent's savage style, and once he had taken his measure, he stood up to him and gave him punch for punch. The mingled din that came from cheek and jaw as they resounded to the blows and from the dreadful grinding of their teeth was like the incessant hammering in a shipyard where planks are being joined and driven home on the reluctant bolts. And they did not cease to punish one another till they were beaten by sheer lack of breath, and drawing a little apart wiped the streams of sweat from their foreheads, gasping in exhaustion. Then they fell upon each other once more, like two bulls tussling in grim rivalry for a fattened heifer. And now Amycus, rising tiptoe like a man felling an ox, stretched up to his full height and brought his heavy fist down on the other. But Polydeuces dodged the blow by a turn of his head, taking the forearm on the edge of his shoulder. Then, closing warily, he landed him a lightning blow above the ear and smashed the bones inside. Amycus collapsed on his knees in agony; the Minyan lords raised a shout of triumph; and in a moment the man was dead.

But the Bebryces did not desert their king; they all picked up their spears and hardened clubs, and charged at Polydeuces. His comrades, however, stood in front of him with their keen swords unsheathed, and Castor drew first blood, smiting the head of a man who rushed at him, with such force that the severed halves fell down on his shoulders right and left. Polydeuces himself dealt with the huge Itymoneus and Mimas. He took a running jump at Itymoneus, kicked him in the wind, and felled him in the dust. Then, as Mimas came in, he struck him with his right hand above the left eyebrow and tore away his eyelid, leaving the eyeball bare. Meanwhile, Oreides, an ill-conditioned bully who had served the king as squire, wounded Talaus in the side, but failed to kill him: the bronze spear passed under his belt but only cut the skin and did not penetrate. So, too, Aretus gave Iphitus, staunch son of Eurytus, a shrewd blow with his hardened club. But Iphitus was not yet doomed to die; it was Aretus who was soon to fall, to Clytius' sword. And now Ancaeus, Lycurgus' valiant son, seized his enormous axe, and holding a black bearskin as a shield on his left arm, hurled himself with fury on the massed foe. Telamon and Peleus dashed in with him and warlike Jason joined the charge.

Picture a great flock of sheep thrown into panic on a winter's day when the grey wolves have fallen on the folds, eluding shepherds and keen-scented dogs alike. There stand the wolves, inspecting their assembled prey and wondering which to pounce on first and carry off, while all that the sheep can do is to huddle in a mass and trample on each other's backs. Such was the terror that the Argonauts inspired in their presumptuous enemies.

These could no longer stand their ground. They scattered like a great swarm of bees when shepherds or bee-keepers smoke them in their rocky hive. For a while there is tumult in the home and an angry buzzing from the crowded bees; then, when the black smoke has done its work, they dart out from the rock and scatter far and wide. So did the Bebryces, fleeing inland and spreading the news of Amycus' death. Meanwhile another unforeseen disaster was upon them. The poor fools did not know that at this very time their vineyards and villages, deserted by their king, were being ravaged by the hostile arms of Lycus and his Mariandyni, a tribe who had fought them time and again for the possession of the iron-bearing land. And the Argonauts were pillaging their cattle-yards and folds, and rounding up large flocks of sheep.

The victors began to wonder what greater cowardice the Bebryces could have displayed if fortune had permitted Heracles himself to meet them. 'Had he been here,' said one young lord, 'there would certainly have been no sparring. The great club would soon have made the king forget his pride and all the rules he came up to proclaim. And that is the man whom we marooned! Now that we have lost him, we shall soon learn one and all what blind fools we have been.' But what he did not know was that the pattern of all these events had been designed by Zeus.

They stayed there through the night, tended their wounded and with an offering to the immortal gods prepared a mighty feast. Nobody fell asleep by the wine-bowl and the blazing sacrifice. They crowned their golden heads with bay from the tree on the shore round which they had cast their hawsers, and in harmony with Orpheus' lyre they sang a song in praise of Polydeuces, Therapnaean son of Zeus. Their music charmed the windless shore.

When the sun came back from the world's end to light the dewy hills and wake the shepherds, they loosed their hawsers from the trunk of the bay-tree, and after stowing in the ship all of their booty that might be of use, they sailed up the swirling Bosporus before the wind. But here there loomed ahead of them a great wave mountain-high, which over-topped the clouds and threatened to engulf them. Full of menace it hung in the sky above the very centre of the ship – they seemed to be inevitably doomed. Yet even so it came to nothing: all that was needed was a good hand at the helm. And so, through the skill of Tiphys, they came away unhurt, though badly frightened; and the next day they brought their ship to rest on the coast that faces the Bithynian land.

Here by the sea was the home of Phineus son of Agenor. Phoebus had once endowed this man with prophetic powers, but the gift had brought on him the most appalling tribulations. For he showed no reverence even for Zeus, whose sacred purposes he did not scruple to disclose in full to all. Zeus punished him for this by giving him a lingering old age, without the boon of sight. He even robbed him of such pleasure as he might have got from the many dainties which neighbours kept bringing to his house when they came there to consult the oracle. On every such occasion the Harpies swooped down through the clouds and snatched the food from his mouth and hands with their beaks, sometimes leaving him not a morsel, sometimes a few scraps, so that he might live and be tormented. They gave a loathsome stench to everything. What bits were left emitted such a smell that no one could have borne to put them in his mouth or even to come near.

But directly Phineus heard the voices and footsteps of the Argonauts he knew that these visitors were the very men at whose arrival Zeus had told him he would once more be permitted to enjoy his food. He rose from his bed, like a phantom in a dream, and with the aid of a staff crept to the door on withered feet, feeling his way along the walls. Weakness and age made his limbs tremble as he walked; his shrivelled flesh was caked with dirt, and his bones were held together only by the skin. When he had come out from the hall, his knees gave way and he sat down on the threshold of the courtyard. And there he swooned. The ground beneath him seemed to reel; and he sank down in a coma without the power to speak or stir.

When the Argonauts saw this, they gathered round him in amazement; and after some time Phineus painfully recovered breath enough to speak and uttered these prophetic words:

'Listen to me, flower of Hellenic chivalry, if you are indeed the crew of *Argo*, led by Jason in quest of the fleece at a cruel king's command. Yes, you are they – knowledge of everything still comes to my prophetic soul, for which I render thanks to you, my Lord Apollo, Leto's Son, crushed though I am beneath a load of suffering. And now, by Zeus the suppliants' god, who is the sternest judge of sinful men, by Phoebus, and by Hera too, whose special favour brought you here, I beseech you to help me, to save a luckless man from degradation and not to pass on unconcernedly and leave me as I am. Not only has the Fury quenched my sight, so that I drag myself through my last years in misery, but over and above all this I am the victim of another curse, which plagues me more than all. Harpies who live in some abominable haunt that lies beyond our ken swoop down on me and snatch the food from my lips. There is nothing I can do to stop them. It would be easier for me, when I am hungry, to forget my appetite than it would be to escape from them, so swiftly do they dart down from the sky. And if they leave me any food at all it stinks of putrefaction, the smell is intolerable, and no one could bear to come near it, even for a moment, even if he had an adamantine will. Yet bitter necessity that cannot be gainsaid, not only keeps me there, but forces me to pamper my accursed belly.

'But there is an oracle which says that these Harpies shall be dealt with by the two sons of the North Wind – no unknown foreigner shall drive them off. That is the truth, if I indeed am Phineus, once famous for his wealth and his prophetic skill, Phineus, Agenor's son, who when he ruled in Thrace won Cleopatra, sister of that pair, with his bridal gifts and brought her to his home.'

Phineus had spoken; and the young lords were all stirred to pity, Zetes and Calaïs more than any. Brushing their tears away these two went up to the sorrowful old man, and Zetes took his hand in his.

'Poor man!' he said. 'I cannot think that anyone on earth has more to bear than you. What is the reason for this persecution? Have you been rash enough to offend the gods by some misuse of your prophetic skill? Is that why they are so angry with you? We should be quick to help you, if it were true that we are destined for this honour. Yet the thought fills us with dismay. No one is left in doubt when Heaven is punishing a mortal man. And for all our eagerness we dare not undertake to foil the Harpies when they come, unless you can assure us on oath that by doing so we shall not lose the favour of the gods.'

The old man opened his sightless eyes, and raising them as though to look him in the face, replied to Zetes:

'Say no more, my child. I beg you not to entertain such fears. I swear by Leto's Son, who of his own accord taught me prophetic lore; by my own ill-starred fate; by the dark cloud that veils my eyes; by the Powers below – and may they blast me if I die forsworn – that you will not incur the wrath of Heaven by helping me.'

Reassured by these oaths, the pair were eager to take up his cause. The younger members of the party immediately prepared a meal for the old man – the last pickings that the Harpies were to get from him – while Zetes and Calaïs took their stand beside him ready to smite them with their swords when they attacked. And Phineus had scarcely taken the first morsel up when, with as little warning as a whirlwind or a lightning flash, they dropped from the clouds proclaiming their desire for food with raucous cries. The young lords saw them coming and raised the alarm. Yet they had hardly done so before the Harpies had devoured the whole meal and were on the wing once more, far out at sea. All they left was an intolerable stench.

Raising their swords, the two sons of the North Wind flew off in pursuit. Zeus gave them indefatigable strength; indeed, without his aid, there could have been no chase, for whenever the Harpies came to Phineus' house or left it they outstripped the storm winds from the West. But Zetes and Calaïs very nearly caught them. They even touched them, though to little purpose, with their finger-tips, like a couple of keen hounds on a hillside, hot on the track of a horned goat or a deer, pressing close behind the quarry and snapping at the empty air. Yet even with Heaven against them, the long chase would certainly have ended in their tearing the Harpies to pieces when they overtook them at the Floating Isles, but for Iris of the Swift Feet, who when she saw them leapt down from Olympus through the sky and checked them with these words:

'Sons of Boreas, you may not touch the Harpies with your swords: they are the hounds of almighty Zeus. But I myself will undertake on oath that never again shall they come near to Phineus.' And she went on to swear by the waters of Styx, the most portentous and inviolable oath that any god can take, that the Harpies should never visit Phineus' house again, such being Fate's decree. This oath prevailed upon the noble brothers, who wheeled round and set their course for safety and the ship; which is the reason why the Floating Isles have changed their name and are now called the Islands of Return. The Harpies and Iris went their different ways. The Harpies withdrew to a den in Minoan Crete, and Iris soared up to Olympus, cleaving the air with her unflagging wings.

Meanwhile the other Argonauts, after washing all the filth from the old man's body, picked out the finest of the sheep they had recently acquired at Amycus' expense and made a sacrifice. Then they set out a splendid banquet in the hall and sat down to enjoy it. Phineus joined them and ate ravenously; he was as happy as a man in a delightful dream. They took their fill of meat and drink and stayed awake all night, waiting for Zetes and Calaïs to return. The old man sat among them by the hearth, and for their benefit rehearsed the stages of their future journey to its very end.

'Listen now,' he said. 'You are not entitled to know every detail, but I will tell you what the gods permit. At one time, in my folly, I was rash enough to disclose the plans of Zeus from start to finish. I now realize that he himself intends a prophet's revelations to be incomplete, so that humanity may miss some part of Heaven's design.

'When you leave me, the first thing you see will be the two Cyanean Rocks, at the end of the straits. To the best of my knowledge, no one has ever made his way between them, for not being fixed to the bottom of the sea they frequently collide, flinging up the water in a seething mass which falls on the rocky flanks of the straits with a resounding roar. Now if, as I take it, you are god-fearing travellers and men of sense, you will be advised by me: you will not rashly throw away your lives or rush into danger with the recklessness of youth. Make an experiment first. Send out a dove from *Argo* to explore the way. If she succeeds in flying in between the Rocks and out across the sea, do not hesitate to follow in her path, but get a firm grip on your oars and cleave the water of the straits. For that is the time when salvation will depend, not on your prayers, but on your strength of arm. So think of nothing else, be firm, and spend your energies on what will pay you best. By all means pray to the gods, but choose an earlier moment. And if the dove flies on, but comes to grief midway, turn back. It is always better to submit to Heaven; and you could not possibly escape a dreadful end. The Rocks would crush you, even if *Argo* were an iron ship. Ah, my poor friends, I do implore you not to disregard my counsel from the gods, even if you imagine their hatred of myself to be far more bitter than in fact it is. Do not dare to sail farther in, if the bird's failure warns you to desist.

'Well, all this will happen as it must. But if you come

safely through the Clashing Rocks into the Black Sea, sail on with the land of the Bithynians on your right, shunning the coastal surf, till you round the mouth of the swift River Rhebas and the Black Cape and come to harbour in the Isle of Thynias. From that point, sail on a little way and beach your ship on the coast of the Mariandyni, which lies opposite. Here there is a path that leads down to Hades' realm, and rising high above it, the promontory of Acherusias, where the swirling waters of Acheron gush up from the very bowels of the rock and pour down to the sea by way of a deep ravine. A little farther on, you will skirt the hilly land of the Paphlagonians, where Eneteian Pelops reigned. He was their first king and the people claim descent from him.

'Opposite Helice the Bear there is a foreland called Carambis, steep on every side and presenting to the sea a lofty pinnacle which splits the wind-stream from the North in two. When you have rounded this, the whole length of Aegialus will lie before you. But at the very end of it the coast juts out, and there the waters of Halys come down with a terrific roar. Near by, the smaller River Iris rolls foaming to the sea; and farther east a great and lofty cape is thrust out from the land. Then comes the mouth of the River Thermodon, which, after wandering across the continent, flows into a quiet bay by the cape of Themiscyra. Here is the plain of Doeas, and the three towns of the Amazons near by. The Chalybes come next, a miserable tribe, whose land is rugged and intractable; but they toil away and work the iron that it yields. Near them live the sheep-farming Tibareni, beyond the Genetaean Cape, sacred to Zeus the strangers' god. Next, and marching with them, are the Mossynoeci. These people occupy the forest lands below the mountains. They build their wooden houses in the form of towers, which they call *mossynes*, taking their own name from their well-constructed homes. When you have left these behind, you must beach your ship on a low-lying island, though not before you find some means of driving off the innumerable birds that haunt the lonely shore and pay no deference to man. Here the Queens of the Amazons, Ottere and Antiope, built a marble shrine for Ares when they were going to war. And here I advise you – and you know I am your friend – to stay a little while; for a godsend will come to you out of the bitter brine. But I must not sin again by telling you in detail all that I myself foresee.

'Beyond the island and the mainland opposite, live the Philyres; beyond them the Macrones; and farther still the numerous tribes of the Becheiri. Next to these live the Sapeires; beyond their borders, the Byzeres; and beyond them again the warlike Colchians themselves. But sail on till you come to the farthest corner of the Black Sea. There, in the land of Cytaïs, a broad river, which comes from the distant Amarantian Mountains over the Circaean plain, rolls swiftly to the sea. This is the Phasis. Drive *Argo* into the marshes at its mouth, and you will see the walls of King Aeetes' city and the dark grove of Ares, where the fleece is spread on the top of an oak, watched over by a serpent, a formidable beast who peers all round and never, night or day, allows sweet sleep to conquer his unblinking eyes.'

His recital left the Argonauts dismayed. There was a

long silence, which the lord Jason was the first to break. He was unmanned by his misgivings.

'Sir,' he said, 'you have rehearsed the hazards of our voyage and brought us to our destination. You have given us the clue for our passage through the hateful Rocks into the Black Sea. But what I also wish to learn from you is whether, after escaping them, we shall get safely back to Hellas. How shall I manage? How am I to find my way once more across that vast expanse of water? My comrades are as inexperienced as I am; and Colchian Aea lies at the far end of the Black Sea and of the world itself.'

'My son,' the old man replied, 'once you have made the passage of the deadly Rocks, fear nothing, for some Power will lead you back from Aea by a different route, and on the outward journey there will be guides enough. But remember this, my friends. You could have no better ally than that artful goddess, Aphrodite. Indeed the happy issue of your venture hangs on her. But question me no more.'

Phineus had scarcely finished when the two sons of Thracian Boreas came swooping from the sky and brought their winged feet to rest on the threshold. The moment they saw them, the whole company leapt from their seats, and Zetes, still panting from exertion, told his eager friends how long the chase had been; how Iris had saved the Harpies' lives, but with a gracious undertaking for the time to come; and how the frightened monsters had taken refuge in the great cavern under the cliff of Dicte. The news delighted everybody in the hall, their own friends as well as Phineus himself, and Jason in all kindness wished him joy.

'There was a god then, after all,' he said, 'who cared for you in your terrible affliction and brought us here from distant lands so that the sons of Boreas might save you. If he should also give you back your sight, I should be as happy as I shall be if I reach my home again.'

But the old man bowed his head in sorrow and replied: 'Lord Jason, my sight is past recall. My eyes are ruined and there is no cure. I pray, instead, for death to take me soon. When I am dead I shall partake of perfect bliss.'

Thus for a little while the two conversed. They were still engaged in talk when the first light of dawn appeared. And now there came to Phineus' house the daily crowd of visitors with their customary offerings from their own larders. The old man had always treated rich and poor with equal courtesy, telling their fortunes and in many cases saving them from evil by his own foreknowledge. No wonder that they came there and looked after him.

On this occasion they were joined by his best friend, Paraebius, who was delighted to find a party of strangers in the house, since Phineus had once told him that a band of noblemen on their way from Hellas to Aeetes' city would come to land on the Thynian coast and with the good will of Zeus put an end to the Harpies' depredations. So now the old man, after satisfying his visitors with sage replies to their enquiries, dismissed them all except Paraebius, whom he invited to stay there with his noble guests. But presently he sent him too away, telling him to come back with the finest of his sheep. And when Paraebius had left the hall he addressed the oarsmen of *Argo* in a gentle voice:

'You see, my friends, that not everyone is graceless or

forgetful of benefits received. I am thinking of Paraebius, who came here just now to have his fortune told. There was a time in that man's life when the more he toiled the harder he found it to keep body and soul together. He sank lower day by day, and there was no respite from his labours. He was paying in misery for a sin committed by his father, who had refused to listen to a Hamadryad's prayers when he was felling trees one day, alone in the mountains. She wished him to spare the stump of an oak which was as old as she and had been her only home for many a long year. She wept and pleaded with him piteously. But in the headstrong arrogance of youth he cut it down; and in revenge the nymph laid a curse on him and his children. When Paraebius consulted me, I realized the nature of the sin and told him to build an altar to the Thynian nymph and there make an offering in atonement, with prayers for release from his father's doom. Thus he escaped the wrath of Heaven, and never since that day has he forgotten or neglected me. Indeed, he is so determined to stand by me in my troubles that I find it very hard to make him leave the house.'

He had no sooner finished than Paraebius reappeared, bringing two of his sheep along with him. At a word from Phineus, Jason and the two sons of Boreas bestirred themselves and, as evening fell, made a sacrifice on the hearth with invocations to Apollo, Lord of Prophecy. The younger men prepared a sumptuous feast, and when all had enjoyed it they lay down to sleep, some by the ship's hawsers, others in groups in various parts of the house.

But at dawn the Etesian Winds were blowing in full

force, as they do throughout the world by an ordinance from Zeus. This is how it came about. Folk say that once upon a time there was a shepherdess called Cyrene who used to graze her flocks in the water-meadows of Peneus. She was a virgin and she prized her maidenhood. But one day when she was tending her sheep down by the river, Apollo carried her off from Haemonia and set her down among the nymphs of the land in distant Libya near the Myrtosian Mount. There she bore him a son called Aristaeus, who is remembered now in the corn-lands of Haemonia as the Hunter and the Shepherd. Cyrene herself was left in Libya by Apollo, who in token of his love made her a nymph and huntress with the gift of a long life. But he took his infant son away to be brought up by Cheiron in his cave. When the child had grown up the divine Muses found him a bride, taught him the arts of healing and prophecy, and made him the shepherd of all their flocks that grazed on the Athamantian plain in Phthia, round Mount Othrys and in the valley of the sacred River Apidanus. There came a time, however, when Aristaeus migrated. The Dog-star Sirius was scorching the Minoan Islands from the sky, and the people could find no permanent cure for the trouble till the Archer-King Apollo put it in their heads to send for Aristaeus. So, at his father's command, Aristaeus assembled the Parrhasian tribe, who are descendants of Lycaon, left Phthia, and settled in Ceos. He raised a great altar to the Rain-god Zeus and made ritual offerings in the hills to the Dog-star and to Zeus himself, the Son of Cronos. In response, Zeus gave his orders – and the Etesian Winds refresh the earth for forty days. The priests of Ceos still make yearly sacrifice before the rising of the Dog.

That is the story of the winds that now detained the Argonauts in Thynia. Every day, to please Phineus, the people sent them generous gifts. In the end the young lords built an altar to the Blessed Twelve on the beach beyond the house and after laying offerings on it, embarked and sat down to the oars. And they did not forget the bird that they must carry with them. Euphemus took the shy dove in his hands and brought her on board, trembling with fright, before they cast their double hawsers off.

Argo's departure did not escape Athene's eye. She promptly took her stand on a cloud which, though light, could bear her formidable weight, and swept down to the sea, filled with concern for the oarsmen in the ship. There comes a moment to the patient traveller (and there are many such that wander far afield) when the road ahead of him is clear and the distance so foreshortened that he has a vision of his home, he sees his way to it over land and sea, and in his fancy travels there and back so quickly that it seems to stand before his eager eyes. Such was Athene's speed as she darted down to set foot on the inhospitable coast of Thynia.

In due course they found themselves entering the narrowest part of the winding straits. Rugged cliffs hemmed them in on either side, and *Argo* as she advanced began to feel a swirling undercurrent. They moved ahead in fear, for now the clash of the colliding Rocks and the thunder of surf on the shores fell ceaselessly on their ears. Euphemus seized the dove and climbed on to the prow, while the oarsmen, at Tiphys' orders, made a special effort, hoping by their own strength of arm to drive *Argo* through the Rocks forthwith. They rounded a bend and saw a thing that no one after them has seen – the Rocks were moving apart. Their hearts sank; but now Euphemus launched the dove on her flight and the eyes of all were raised to watch her as she passed between the Rocks.

Once more the Rocks met face to face with a resounding crash, flinging a great cloud of spray into the air. The sea gave a terrific roar and the broad sky rang again. Caverns underneath the crags bellowed as the sea came surging in. A great wave broke against the cliffs and the white foam swept high above them. *Argo* was spun round as the flood reached her.

But the dove got through, unscathed but for the tips of her tail-feathers, which were nipped off by the Rocks. The oarsmen gave a cry of triumph and Tiphys shouted at them to row with all their might, for the Rocks were opening again. So they rowed on full of dread, till the backwash, overtaking them, thrust *Argo* in between the Rocks. Then the fears of all were turned to panic. Sheer destruction hung above their heads.

They had already reached a point where they could see the vast sea opening out on either side, when they were suddenly faced by a tremendous billow arched like an overhanging rock. They bent their heads down at the sight, for it seemed about to fall and overwhelm the ship. But Tiphys just in time checked her as she plunged forward, and the great wave slid under her keel. Indeed it raised her stern so high in the air that she was carried clear of the Rocks. Euphemus ran along shouting to all his friends to put their backs into their rowing, and with answering shouts they struck the water. Yet for every foot that *Argo* made she lost two, though the oars bent like curved bows as the men put out their strength.

But now another overhanging wave came rushing down on them, and when *Argo* had shot end-on like a rolling-pin through the hollow lap of this terrific sea, she found herself held back by the swirling tide just in the place where the Rocks met. To right and left they shook and rumbled; but *Argo* could not budge.

This was the moment when Athene intervened. Holding on to the hard rock with her left hand, she pushed the ship through with the other; and *Argo* clove the air like a winged arrow, though even so the Rocks, clashing in their accustomed way, sheared off the tip of the mascot on the stern. When the men had thus got through unhurt, Athene soared up to Olympus. But the Rocks were now rooted for ever in one spot close to one another. It had been decided by the happy gods that this should be their fate when a human being had seen them and sailed through. The Argonauts, freed from the cold grip of panic, breathed again when they saw the sky once more and the vast ocean stretching out ahead. They felt that they had come through Hell alive.

Tiphys was the first to speak. 'I think,' he said, 'that we can say all's well. *Argo* is safe and so are we. And for that, to whom are we indebted but Athene, who endowed the ship with supernatural strength when Argus drove the bolts home in her planks? *Argo* shall not be caught; that seems to be a law. And so, Lord Jason, now that Heaven has allowed us to pass safely through the Rocks, I beg you not to dread so much the duty that your king assigned you. Has not Phineus told us that from now on we shall meet no obstacle we cannot easily surmount?'

Tiphys, with that, steered straight across the open sea along the Bithynian coast. But Jason, for his own purposes, took him gently to task. 'Tiphys,' he said, 'why do you try to comfort me in my distress? I was blind and made a fatal error. When Pelias ordered me to undertake this mission, I ought to have refused outright, even though he would have torn me limb from limb without compunction. But as things are, I am obsessed by fears and intolerable anxiety, hating the thought of the cruel sea that we must cross and of what may happen when we land and find the natives hostile, as we are sure to do at every point. Ever since you all rallied to my side these cares have occupied my mind, and when each day is done I spend the night in misery. It is easy for you, Tiphys, to talk in a cheerful vein. You are only concerned for your own life, whereas I care nothing for mine, but *am* concerned for each and all alike, you and the rest of my friends. How can I tell whether I shall bring you safely back to Hellas?'

Jason's speech, which was designed to put his noble comrades to the test, met with acclamation. His heart was warmed by their reassuring cries and he spoke again, this time with greater candour. 'My friends, your courage fills me with fresh confidence. The resolution that you show in face of awful perils makes me feel that I could go through Hell itself and fear nothing. However, now that we have left the Clashing Rocks behind us I have no reason to expect another such ordeal, provided that we keep to the course laid down for us by Phineus.'

This ended the discussion and they now devoted all their energies to rowing. Before long they passed the swift River Rhebas and the peak of Colone, and soon after that the Black Cape, and then the outfall of the River Phyllis. It was here that Phrixus son of Athamas had been entertained by Dipsacus when he was flying with his ram from the city of Orchomenus. This Dipsacus was the son of a meadow-nymph and the River Phyllis. He was an unassuming person who was quite content to live with his mother by his father's stream and graze his flocks beside the sea. The Argonauts could see, as they passed them in turn, his shrine, and the broad banks of the river, and the plain, and the deep stream of Calpe; and all that day and through the windless night they laboured at the indefatigable oar. They worked like oxen ploughing the moist earth. The sweat pours down from flank and neck; their rolling eyes glare out askance from under the yoke; hot blasts of breath come rumbling from their mouths; and all day long they labour, digging their hoofs into the soil. Thus the crew of *Argo* all through the night ploughed the salt water with their oars.

But at that time of day when heavenly light has not yet come, nor is there utter darkness, but the faint glimmer that we call twilight spreads over the night and wakes us, they ran into the harbour of the lonely isle of Thynias and went ashore exhausted by their labours. Here they had a vision of Apollo on his way from Lycia to visit the remote and teeming peoples of the North.

The golden locks streamed down his cheeks in clusters as he moved; he had a silver bow in his left hand and a quiver slung on his back; the island quaked beneath his feet and the sea ran high on the shore. They were awestruck at the sight and no one dared to face the god and meet his lovely eyes. They stood there with bowed heads while he, aloof, passed through the air on his way across the sea.

Orpheus found his voice at last. 'Come now,' he said to the Argonauts, 'let us dedicate this island to Apollo of the Dawn and call it by that name, since it was here that we all saw him pass by in the dawn. We will build an altar on the shore and make such offerings as we have at our command. Later, if he grants us a safe return to Haemonia, we will sacrifice to him the thighs of horned goats. Now, let us propitiate him as best we can, with libations and the scent of burnt-offerings. Lord of the Vision, look kindly upon us.'

They set to work at once. Some built an altar with shingle, while others explored the island in the hope of catching sight of a fawn or a wild goat. Its forest pastures promised well, and with the aid of Leto's Son they found their game. Then, with due ritual, they wrapped all the thigh bones in fat, burnt them on the sacred altar with invocations to Apollo of the Dawn and danced in a wide ring round the burning sacrifice singing 'Glory to Phoebus; glory to the Healing God!' The lord Orpheus joined them in their worship. Striking his Bistonian lyre, he told them in song how Apollo long ago, when he was still a beardless youth rejoicing in his locks, slew the monster Delphyne with his bow beneath the rocky brow of Parnassus. 'Be gracious to us, King,' he sang, 'and may thy tresses for ever be unshorn, intact for ever! That is their due, the locks that only Leto strokes with her fond hands.' And he sang to them of the daughters of Pleistus, the Corycian Nymphs, who had encouraged the god by their repeated cry of 'Healer'. 'That,' he told them, 'is the origin of the beautiful refrain with which you have been hymning Phoebus.'

When the Argonauts had worshipped the god with dance and song, they made holy libations and touching the sacrifice as they swore took an oath to stand by one another in unity for ever. A temple of Concord can be seen on the spot to this very day. They built it themselves in honour of the glorious goddess.

With dawn on the third day there came a fresh west wind, and they left the lofty island. Skirting the mainland coast, they saw in turn the mouth of the River Sangarius, the fertile lands of the Mariandyni, the River Lycus and the Anthemoeisian lagoon. The ship's halyards and all the other tackle quivered in the wind as they sped along; but during the night the breeze dropped, and with thankful hearts they made harbour at dawn by the Cape of Acherusias. This lofty headland, with its sheer cliffs, looks out across the Bithynian Sea. Beneath it at sea level lies a solid platform of smooth rock on which the rollers break and roar, while high up on the very summit plane trees spread out their branches. On the landward side it falls away in a hollow glen. Here is the Cavern of Hades with its overhanging trees and rocks, from the chill depths of which an icy breath comes up and each morning covers everything with sparkling rime that melts under the midday sun. The frowning headland is never visited by silence; a murmur from the sounding sea mingles for ever with the rustling of the leaves as they are shaken by the winds from Hades' Cave.

Here too is the mouth of the River Acheron, which issues from the mountainside and falls, by way of a deep ravine, into the eastern sea. On a later occasion the Megarians of Nisaea, when on their way to settle in the land of the Mariandyni, had good reason to call this river the Sailors' Saviour: the harbour at its mouth saved them and their ships when they were caught in a violent gale. The Argonauts brought their ship to the same spot. Shortly after the wind had dropped, they beached her in the shelter of the Acherusian Cape.

Lycus, the local chieftain, and his Mariandyni soon got word of their arrival. These were surely the slayers of Amycus – so much they had already heard. And it was quite enough; they made a league with them forthwith. As for Polydeuces, they flocked in from every side to welcome him as a god, bearing in mind their own long struggles with the insolent Bebryces. Then they all went up to the city like good friends and spent the day in feasting and agreeable talk in the palace of Lycus. Jason gave him the name and lineage of each of his men, and after explaining his mission went on to tell him of the welcome they had had from the Lemnian women, and of their dealings with the Doliones of Cyzicus; how they reached Mysia and Cius, where much against their will they had left the noble Heracles; of Glaucus's advice; of the slaying of Amycus and his men, the afflictions and prophecies of Phineus, their escape from the Cyanean

Rocks, and their meeting with Apollo on the island. Lycus was enthralled by the tale, but he grieved for the abandoned Heracles and spoke of him, addressing all the Argonauts:

'My friends, what a powerful ally you have lost for the rest of your long journey to Colchis. I say this because I well remember seeing him in my father Dascylus's palace when he had come to us overland on foot with the belt of the fighting Amazon Hippolyte. I was a lad then with the first down on my cheeks. Some Mysians had killed my brother Priolas, whom the people still lament with the most piteous dirges, and at the funeral games Heracles beat the great boxer Titias, the finest and most powerful of our youths – he knocked out all his teeth. Then he subdued for my father, not only the Mysians, but the Phrygians whose fields march with ours, and also the Bithynian tribes, conquering their lands as far as the mouth of the Rhebas and the peak of Colone. After which, Pelops's Paphlagonians, those whose land is scoured by the dark waters of Billaeus, gave in to him without a blow.

'But now that Heracles is far away the Bebryces and their brutal king have long been preying on me. They have cut off large parcels of my land, thrusting their frontier right up to the meadows watered by the deep River Hypius. However, they have paid the price through you. Indeed I think that Heaven had a hand in things that day when Tyndareus' son killed Amycus and so provoked the Bebryces to fight. And I am most willing to repay you by any means within my power. It is only proper that the weak should recompense the strong when they take steps to help them. So now I shall ask Dascylus, my son, to join you in your enterprise. With him on board you will encounter none but friends on your voyage, up to the mouth of the Thermodon itself. Not only that, but I propose to build high up on the Acherusian Cape a great temple to the sons of Tyndareus for sailors out at sea to mark and reverence; and then I will dedicate to them, as gods, some rich acres of the fertile plain outside the town.'

All that day they feasted and made merry; but at dawn they hurried down to the ship. Lycus himself went with them. He had loaded them with countless gifts and he brought his son from home to sail with them.

But at this moment Fate intervened and Idmon son of Abas met his predestined end. He was a learned soothsayer, but not all his prophetic lore could save him now: he had to die. In the water-meadow by a reedy stream there lay a white-tusked boar cooling his flanks and huge belly in the mud. This evil brute, who was feared even by the meadow-sprites, lived all alone in the wide fen, and no one was the wiser. But now, as Idmon made his way along the dykes of the muddy river, the boar leapt out of some hidden lair in the reeds, charged at him and gashed his thigh, severing the sinews and the bone itself. Idmon fell to the ground with a sharp cry. The others gave their stricken friend an answering shout, and Peleus quickly aimed his javelin at the murderous boar as he beat his retreat into the fen. The beast turned and charged again. But this time Idas wounded him, and with a loud grunt he fell impaled on the well-aimed spear. They left him where he fell, but they carried

Idmon, who was at his last gasp, to the ship with heavy hearts; and he died in his friends' arms.

All thoughts of sailing were abandoned; they waited there in sorrow for the funeral of their friend. For three days they mourned him and on the fourth they buried him with signal honours. The people and King Lycus himself took part in the rites, and when they had laid him in the earth they slaughtered many sheep, as is a dead man's due. A barrow too was raised near by in the hero's honour, bearing a monument that may still be seen in these latter days, the trunk of a wild olive big enough to make a roller for a ship. It is still alive and putting out its leaves not far below the Acherusian height. But if the whole story must be told (and here I am guided by the Muse), although Apollo strictly commanded the Boeotians and Nisaeans to revere Idmon as the guardian of their settlement and build their town round the trunk of this old olive, they venerate Agamestor to this very day instead of Idmon the god-fearing Aeolid.

Meanwhile the Argonauts soon had to build a second barrow for another comrade dead: two monuments still mark the place. Who then was the next to die? The story goes that it was Tiphys son of Hagnias whom Destiny allowed to sail no farther. There on the spot, far from his home, a short illness laid him to rest while the company paid funeral honours to the son of Abas. Their grief at this catastrophe was profound, and when they had buried him also, close to the other, they cast themselves down by the sea in despair and lay there wrapped up like figures cut in stone, without a word and with no thought of food or drink. There was no spirit left in them; all hope of finding their way back was gone, and they might have stayed there in their grief still longer, had not the goddess Hera filled Ancaeus with the courage that dares all. This man was a son of the Sea-god, borne to him by Astypalaea near the waters of Imbrasus, and steersmanship was his especial skill. He ran up to Peleus and said:

'My lord, what sense is there in giving up the quest and wasting time in this outlandish spot? Jason brought me all the way from Parthenia to help him find the fleece, not because I am a fighter, but because I do know something about ships. So believe me, you need have no fears at all for *Argo*. And I am not the only one; there are others here who know the sea. Not one of them would lead us into trouble if we put him at the helm. I beg you to pass all this on at once and to remind them boldly of their duty.'

Peleus' heart leapt up for joy and he quickly summoned the others. 'My friends,' he said, 'why indulge in this unprofitable grief? When our two comrades died, that must have been their destiny. But we have other steersmen with us, plenty of them. On, then, with our adventure; there is no excuse for loitering. Wake up, I say, and work, casting your sorrows to the winds.'

But Jason took him up; he could see no light ahead. 'My lord Peleus,' he said, 'where are these pilots of yours? The seamen whom we used to count on are even more despondent and unmanned than I am. Indeed, I see nothing for us but a fate as sad as that of our lost friends. For it looks as though we should neither reach the terrible Aeetes' city nor find our way back to Hellas past the Clashing Rocks. No, we are doomed to grow old here, inglorious and obscure, with nothing done.'

In spite of this, Ancaeus, inspired by Heaven, promptly undertook to steer the gallant ship. Erginus, too, and Nauplius and Euphemus all stood up, eager to have the task. But their comrades held them back as the greater number voted for Ancaeus.

At dawn on the twelfth day a fresh breeze was blowing from the west. So they went on board, rowed swiftly out from the mouth of the Acheron, and then shook out their sail to the wind and forged ahead through clear weather under a broad spread of canvas. They soon came to the mouths of the River Callichorus, where we are told that Dionysus Son of Zeus, when he had left the Indians and was on his way to Thebes, established revels, with dances in front of a cave, in which he himself passed holy and unsmiling nights. Ever since then, the people of the place have called the stream the River of the Lovely Dance, and the cave the Bedchamber.

Next they saw the tomb of Sthenelus son of Actor, who had joined Heracles in his daring attack on the Amazons, and on the way back had died on the beach from an arrow wound. They paused here, for the goddess Persephone sent up to them the mourning ghost of Actor's son, who craved to see some men of his own kind, if only for a moment. He stood on the edge of his barrow and gazed at the ship, appearing to them in his warlike panoply, with the light flashing from the four plates and purple crest of the fine helmet that he used to wear. Then he sank down again into the great abyss.

The Argonauts were awestruck at the sight, and Mopsus, speaking as their seer, told them to land and with libations lay the ghost. So they quickly brailed the sail, cast hawsers on the shore, and paid honour to the tomb of Sthenelus. They made libations to him and sacrificed some sheep as offerings to the dead. Then, in a separate place, they built an altar to Apollo, Saver of Ships, and burnt the thigh-bones of the sheep. Orpheus made an offering of his own. He dedicated a lyre, in memory of which the place is still called Lyra.

When this was done, as the wind was blowing hard, they re-embarked, let down the sail and drew it taut with both sheets. And *Argo* sped eagerly over the sea, like a high-flying hawk that has set its pinions to the breeze, and flapping them no more glides swiftly on across the sunny sky with wings at rest. They were soon past the spot where the Parthenius flows out to sea; a gentle river this, in whose delectable waters Artemis refreshes herself before ascending to heaven after the chase. Then they pressed on in the night without a stop, passing Sesamus and the crests of Erythini, Crobialus, Cromna, and wooded Cytorus. At sunrise they rounded Cape Carambis, and all that day and on through the night they rowed *Argo* along the endless shores of Aegialus.

They landed on the Assyrian coast, where Zeus himself had once given a home to Sinope daughter of Asopus, granting her the boon of virginity. He was trapped by his own promise. In his passion for the girl he had solemnly sworn to fulfil her dearest wish, whatever that might be; and she very cleverly had said, 'I wish to remain a virgin.' By the same ruse she outwitted Apollo when he made love to her; and the River-god Halys as well. Men fared no better than the gods; this woman never was possessed by any lover.

On the coast here, Deïleon, Autolycus, and Phlogius (sons of the admirable Deïmachus of Tricca) had been living ever since they lost touch with Heracles. When they saw the party land from *Argo* and observed their rank, they approached them, told them who they were and expressed a wish to leave the place for good. They were taken on board at once, as the North-West Wind brooked no delay; and the Argonauts, with these recruits, were carried along by the fresh breeze, leaving behind them the River Halys, its neighbour the Iris, and the delta-land of Assyria. On the same day they rounded the distant headland that guards the harbour of the Amazons. It was here that Melanippe daughter of Ares, having sallied out one day, was caught in an ambush by the great Heracles, though he let her go unharmed when her sister Hippolyte gave him her own resplendent girdle by way of ransom. And here in the bay beyond the cape, as the sea was getting rough, the Argonauts ran ashore at the mouth of the Thermodon.

There is no river like the Thermodon, none that divides itself into so many branches – only four short of a hundred, if you care to count them all. Yet the real headwater is a single stream which flows down to the lowlands from mountains called the Amazonian Heights, and then on through hilly country, which causes it to follow tortuous ways. Separate streams, at varying distances, meander here and there, each seeking its own easiest way to lower levels. Many of these are swallowed up and end without a name. But there is no mistaking the parent river when, rejoined by a few of them, it bursts with an arching crest of foam into the Inhospitable Sea.

Had the Argonauts stayed here as they intended and come to grips with the Amazons, the fight would have been a bloody one. For the Amazons of the Doeantian plain were by no means gentle, well-conducted folk; they were brutal and aggressive, and their main concern in life was war. War, indeed, was in their blood, daughters of Ares as they were and of the Nymph Harmonia, who lay with the god in the depths of the Acmonian Wood and bore him girls who fell in love with fighting.

But Zeus once more sent forth the North-West Wind, and with its help the Argonauts stood out from the curving shore where the Amazons of Themiscyra were arming for battle. I must explain that the Amazons did not all live in one city; there were three separate tribes settled in different parts of the country. The party on the beach, whose queen at that time was Hippolyte, were Themiscyreans. The Lycastians lived apart, and so did the Chadesians, who were javelin-throwers.

At nightfall on the following day they reached the land of the Chalybes. These people do not use the ploughing ox. They not only grow no corn, but plant no vines or trees for their delicious fruit and graze no flocks in dewy pastures. Their task is to dig for iron in the stubborn ground and they live by selling the metal they produce. To them no morning ever brings a holiday. In a black atmosphere of soot and smoke they live a life of unremitting toil.

Soon after leaving them behind, the Argonauts

rounded the headland of Genetaean Zeus and sailed in safety past the country of the Tibareni. Here, when a woman is in childbirth, it is the husband who takes to his bed. He lies there groaning with his head wrapped up and his wife feeds him with loving care. She even prepares the bath for the event.

Next they passed the Sacred Mountain and the highlands where the Mossynoeci live in the *mossynes* or wooden houses from which they take their name. These people have their own ideas of what is right and proper. What we as a rule do openly in town or market-place they do at home; and what we do in the privacy of our houses they do out of doors in the open street, and nobody thinks the worse of them. Even the sexual act puts no one to the blush in this community. On the contrary, like swine in the fields, they lie down on the ground in promiscuous intercourse and are not at all disconcerted by the presence of others. Then again, their king sits in the loftiest hut of all to dispense justice to his numerous subjects. But if the poor man happens to make a mistake in his findings, they lock him up and give him nothing to eat for the rest of the day.

They left these behind them. And now a day of rowing (since the light wind dropped in the night) had brought them almost abreast of Ares' Isle, when they suddenly beheld one of the War-god's birds, which haunt the island, darting through the air. Flapping its wings over the moving ship it dropped a pointed feather down upon her. The plume struck the left shoulder of the noble Oïleus, who let his oar fall at the sudden blow, while the rest looked in amazement at the winged dart. But

Eribotes, whose seat was next to his, pulled the feather out, took off the band on which his scabbard hung, and bound up the wound. Then, as though one bird had not sufficed, they saw another swooping in. But this time the lord Clytius son of Eurytus was ready with his bow bent. He let fly an arrow, struck the bird, and brought it spinning down beside the gallant ship. Whereupon Amphidamas son of Aleus was moved to address his friends.

'We are close,' he said, 'to the island of Ares. You can tell by these birds. But as I see it, arrows will not help us much when we try to disembark. If you mean to land, we must remember Phineus' warning and think of some better plan. Why, Heracles himself, when he came to Arcadia, was unable with bow and arrow to drive away the birds that swam on the Stymphalian Lake. I saw the thing myself. What he did was to take his stand on a height and make a din by shaking a bronze rattle; and the astounded birds flew off into the distance screeching for fear. We must take our cue from him. I myself have had an idea which I should like to put to you. I suggest that you should all set your crested helmets on your heads and take it in turns, one half to row, the others to protect the ship with their polished spears and shields. Then the whole company must raise a most terrific shout, so that the birds may be scared away by a noise that will be new to them, as well as by the nodding crests and above them your uplifted spears. When we reach the island, if we make it, you can raise a tremendous racket by banging on your shields.'

His sensible suggestion pleased them all, and they put

their helmets on their heads; the glinting bronze and the purple crests waving on top were enough to frighten anyone. Then half the crew rowed in turn while the others covered up the ship with their spears and shields. Locking the shields together, they roofed her over, as a man roofs his house with firmly fitted overlapping tiles, both to add to its beauty and keep out the rain. And the shout that went up from the ship was like the roar that comes from battling armies when the lines charge and meet. However, they did not see a single bird till they reached the island and banged on their shields. Then the birds in their thousand rose into the air and after fluttering about in panic, discharged a heavy shower of feathery darts at the ship as they beat a hasty retreat over the sea towards the mainland hills. But the Argonauts sat there in comfort, like people in a town on which the Son of Cronos has discharged a hail-storm from the clouds. They hear the hail-stones rattle on their roofs, but they do not worry. The stormy season has not caught them unprepared: they have roofed their houses well.

Now you may ask what Phineus had in mind when he advised this princely company to put in at such a place. What could they hope to get by landing there?

On the very day of their arrival it happened that the sons of Phrixus were close by. They had left King Aeetes and were on their way to the city of Orchomenus in a Colchian ship. Their purpose was to recover their grandfather's rich possessions. He himself had told them on his death-bed to undertake the voyage. But Zeus had roused the North Wind to show his might, and signalled by a downpour the rainy advent of Arcturus. All day

Boreas blew softly through the topmost branches of the mountain trees and scarcely stirred the leaves. But at nightfall he fell on the sea with tremendous force and raised the billows with his shrieking blasts. A dark mist blotted out the sky; not a star showed through the clouds; on all sides nothing but impenetrable murk. The sons of Phrixus, drenched and quaking for their lives, were carried along at the mercy of the waves. But now the fury of the wind tore away their sail and split the battered hull in two. However, all four men, promoted by the gods, managed to get hold of a huge beam, one of the many firmly bolted timbers that were scattered when the ship broke up; and wind and waves were driving them towards the island more dead than alive, when a sudden and terrific rain-storm added to their troubles. It lashed the sea, the island, and all of the mainland opposite that was occupied by the savage Mossynoeci. But at last, in the murky night, the driving billows flung the sons of Phrixus and their mighty beam on the island beach; and the floods of rain from Zeus ceased as the sun rose.

The two parties soon approached and met each other. Argus son of Phrixus was the first to speak. 'Whoever you may be,' he said to the Argonauts, 'we beseech you by all-seeing Zeus to treat us kindly and help us in our need. A gale at sea has shattered all the timbers of the wretched craft in which we were sailing on a business venture. So now, throwing ourselves on your mercy, we beg you to let us have something to put on, and to look after us out of pity for men of your own age who have met with disaster. Have some regard for suppliants and strangers, for the sake of Zeus who is their god.

All suppliants and strangers belong to Zeus. And we ourselves, I have no doubt, are in his watchful care.'

In answer, Jason, who saw here the fulfilment of one of Phineus' prophecies, questioned the man closely. 'We shall be glad,' he said, 'to provide at once for all your needs. But first be so good as to tell me where you come from and what business has brought you overseas. And let me know your noble names and pedigrees.'

Argus, though his sufferings had left him dazed, was able to reply: 'You must surely have heard how an Aeolid called Phrixus came to Aea from Hellas. He reached Aeetes' city on the back of a ram which Hermes had turned into gold – you can still see its fleece, spread on the leafy branches of an oak. Phrixus sacrificed the ram at its own suggestion to Zeus alone, because he is the god of fugitives; and Aeetes made him welcome in his palace and married him in all good will to his daughter Chalciope without exacting the usual gifts. Those two were our parents. Phrixus grew old and died in the palace of Aeetes; and now we are carrying out his wishes by travelling to Orchomenus to take possession of our grandfather Athamas's estate. But you also wished to know our names. This then is Cytissorus; this, Phrontis; and this, Melas. My own name is Argus.'

Such was his story; and while the Argonauts, amazed and delighted at this meeting, attended to the shipwrecked men, Jason took up the tale and brought it to a fit conclusion.

'So now we know!' he said. 'You that are begging us to befriend you in your plight are kinsmen of mine on my father's side. Cretheus and Athamas were brothers;

and I am a grandson of Cretheus, travelling like Phrixus from Hellas to Aeetes' city with these companions. But we will go into all this later. First put something on. It must indeed have been the gods who brought you to me in your need.'

With that, he gave them clothing from the ship, and then the whole party made their way to the temple of Ares to sacrifice some sheep, and quickly took their places round the altar. It was made of small stones and stood outside the temple, which had no roof. But inside, a black rock was fixed in the ground. This was sacred, and all the Amazons used at times to pray to it. But it was not their custom, when they came over from the mainland, to make burnt-offerings of sheep or oxen on this altar. Instead, they used the flesh of horses. They kept great herds of them.

When the company had sacrificed, prepared their feast, and eaten, the lord Jason rose and addressed the sons of Phrixus. 'Zeus,' he began, 'is the all-seeing god. Sooner or later we god-fearing men, we that uphold the right, are sure to catch his eye. See first how he rescued your father from a murderous stepmother, making him a rich man besides; and then how he saved you also and brought you unharmed through a terrible storm. And now you have the chance, on board our ship, of travelling east or west, whichever you prefer, either to Aea or to the rich city of divine Orchomenus – a ship, mind you, built with the help of Argus by Athene herself of timber she had felled with her bronze axe on Pelion. In any case, your own ship has been smashed to pieces by the angry sea. She never even reached the Rocks that all day long keep clashing in the straits. That being so, will you not help us in your turn by joining us in our endeavour to bring the golden fleece to Hellas and serving as our pilots on the way? After all, it is my mission to atone for the intended sacrifice of Phrixus, the cause of Zeus's wrath against the Aeolids.'

He spoke persuasively, but they were left aghast. They thought it most unlikely that Aeetes would prove affable when they sought to carry off the ram's fleece. And Argus, who had no desire to be involved in any such adventure, replied:

'My friends, you may rely upon us without fail to help you as best we can in any time of trouble. But I do dread the idea of sailing with you now, for Aeetes has it in his power to be a deadly and relentless enemy. He claims to be a son of Helios; his Colchian tribesmen are innumerable; and his terrifying voice and powerful build might well be envied by the god of war himself. No, it would be no easy thing to take the fleece without permission of Aeetes, guarded as it is from every side by such a serpent, a deathless and unsleeping beast, offspring of Earth herself. She brought him forth on the slopes of Caucasus by the rock of Typhaon. It was there, they say, that Typhaon, when he had offered violence to Zeus and been struck by his thunder-bolt, dropped warm blood from his head, and so made his way to the mountains and plain of Nysa, where he lies to this day, engulfed in the waters of the Serbonian Lake.'

When they heard what an ordeal lay before them, the cheeks of many of his listeners grew pale. But Peleus soon gave Argus a spirited reply.

'My good sir,' he said, 'do not give way to such excessive fears. We are not after all so feeble as to be no match for Aeetes if it comes to a fight. He will be meeting men whom I believe to know as much of war as he does; men too who are not unrelated to the happy gods. And I am confident that if he does not give us the golden fleece of his own free will his Colchian tribes will be of little use to him.'

The two men continued their debate in this fashion till at last, satisfied with their supper, the company retired to rest. When they woke at dawn a gentle breeze was blowing. They raised the sail; it opened to the wind; and soon they had left the Isle of Ares far behind them.

By nightfall they were passing the Isle of Philyra. This was where Cronos son of Uranus, deceiving his consort Rhea, lay with Philyra daughter of Ocean in the days when he ruled the Titans in Olympus and Zeus was still a child, tended in the Cretan cave by the Curetes of Ida. But Cronos and Philyra were surprised in the very act by the goddess Rhea. Whereupon Cronos leapt out of bed and galloped off in the form of a long-maned stallion, while Philyra in her shame left the place, deserting her old haunts, and came to the long Pelasgian ridges. There she gave birth to the monstrous Cheiron, half horse and half divine, the offspring of a lover in a questionable shape.

From there they sailed on past the Macrones and the far-flung lands of the Becheiri, past the truculent Sapeires, past the Byzeres, forging ahead with all the speed that a light wind gave them. And now the last recess of the Black Sea opened up and they caught sight of the high

crags of Caucasus, where Prometheus stood chained by
every limb to the hard rock with fetters of bronze, and
fed an eagle on his liver. The bird kept eagerly returning
to its feed. They saw it in the afternoon flying high above
the ship with a strident whirr. It was near the clouds, yet
it made all their canvas quiver to its wings as it beat by.
For its form was not that of an ordinary bird: the long
quill-feathers of each wing rose and fell like a bank of
polished oars. Soon after the eagle had passed, they heard
Prometheus shriek in agony as it pecked at his liver. The
air rang with his screams till at length they saw the flesh-
devouring bird fly back from the mountain by the same
way as it came.

Night fell, and presently, under the guidance of Argus,
they reached the broad estuary of Phasis, where the
Black Sea ends. They quickly lowered sail and yard and
stowed them in the mast-cage; next they let down the
mast itself to lie beside them; and then rowed straight
up into the mighty river, which rolled in foam to either
bank as it made way for *Argo*'s prow. On their left hand
they had the lofty Caucasus and the city of Aea, on their
right the plain of Ares and the god's sacred grove, where
the snake kept watch and ward over the fleece, spread
on the leafy branches of an oak. The lord Jason himself
poured into the river from a golden cup libations of
pure wine sweet as honey, to Earth, to the gods of the
land, and to the spirits of its famous sons. He besought
them of their grace to give him friendly help and happy
anchorage.

And now Ancaeus said: 'We have reached the land of
Colchis and the River Phasis. It is time for us to consider

whether to speak Aeetes fair or to find some other way of getting what we want.'

Jason, advised by Argus, told his men to row into the reedy marshes and moor the ship with anchor-stones in a spot where she could ride. They found the place a little farther on, and there they passed the rest of the night, waiting for Dawn, who soon appeared to their expectant eyes.

Come, Erato, come lovely Muse, stand by me and take up the tale. How did Medea's passion help Jason to bring back the fleece to Iolcus? You that share Aphrodite's powers must surely know; you that fill virgin hearts with love's inquietude and bear a name that speaks of love's delights.

We left the young lords lying there concealed among the rushes. But ambushed though they were, Hera and Athene saw them and at once withdrew from Zeus and the rest of the immortal gods into a private room to talk the matter over.

Hera began by sounding Athene. 'Daughter of Zeus,' she said, 'let me hear you first. What are we to do? Will you think of some ruse that might enable them to carry off Aeetes' golden fleece to Hellas? Or should they speak him fair in the hope of winning his consent? I know the man is thoroughly intractable. But all the same, no method of approach should be neglected.'

'Hera,' said Athene quickly, 'you have put to me the very questions I have been turning over in my mind. But I must admit that, though I have racked my brains, I have failed so far to think of any scheme that might commend itself to the noble lords.'

For a while the two goddesses sat staring at the floor, each lost in her own perplexities. Hera was the first to break the silence; an idea had struck her. 'Listen,' she said. 'We must have a word with Aphrodite. Let us go together and ask her to persuade her boy, if that is possible, to loose an arrow at Aeetes' daughter, Medea of the many spells, and make her fall in love with Jason. I am sure that with her help he will succeed in bearing off the fleece to Hellas.'

This solution of their problem pleased Athene, who smilingly replied: 'Sprung as I am from Zeus, I have never felt the arrows of the Boy, and of love-charms I know nothing. However, if you yourself are satisfied with the idea, I will certainly go with you. But when we meet her you must be the one to speak.'

The two goddesses rose at once and made their way to the palace of Aphrodite, which her lame consort Hephaestus had built for her when he took her as his bride from the hands of Zeus. They entered the court-yard and paused below the veranda of the room where the goddess slept with her lord and master. Hephaestus himself had gone early to his forge and anvils in a vast cavern on a floating island, where he used to turn out all kinds of curious metalwork with the aid of fire and bellows; and Cypris, left at home alone, was sitting on an inlaid chair which faced the door. She had let her hair fall down on her white shoulders and was combing it with a golden comb before plaiting the long tresses. But when she saw the goddesses outside she stopped and called them in; and she rose to meet them and settled them in easy chairs before resuming her own seat. Then she bound up the uncombed locks with both hands, gave her visitors a smile, and spoke with mock humility:

'Ladies, you honour me! What brings you here after so long? We have seen little of you in the past. To what then do I owe a visit from the greatest goddesses of all?'

'This levity of yours,' said Hera, 'is ill-timed. We two are facing a disaster. At this very moment the lord Jason and his friends are riding at anchor in the River Phasis. They have come to fetch the fleece, and since the time for action is at hand, we are gravely concerned for all of them, particularly Aeson's son. For him, I am prepared to fight with all my might and main, and I will save him, even if he sails to Hell to free Ixion from his brazen chains. For I will not have King Pelias boasting that he has escaped his evil doom, insolent Pelias, who left me out when he made offerings to the gods. Besides which I have been very fond of Jason ever since the time when I was putting human charity on trial and as he came home from the chase he met me at the mouth of the Anaurus. The river was in spate, for all the mountains and their high spurs were under snow and cataracts were roaring down their sides. I was disguised as an old woman and he took pity on me, lifted me up, and carried me across the flood on his shoulders. For that, I will never cease to honour him. But Pelias will not be brought to book for his outrageous conduct unless you yourself make it possible for Jason to return.'

Hera had finished; but for a time words failed the Lady of Cyprus. The sight of Hera begging her for favours struck her with awe; and her answer when it came was gracious. 'Queen of goddesses,' she said, 'regard me as the meanest creature in the world if I fail you in your need. Whatever I can say or do, whatever strength these feeble hands possess, is at your service. Moreover I expect no recompense.'

Hera, choosing her words with care, replied: 'We are not asking you to use your hands: force is not needed. All we require of you is quietly to tell your boy to use his wizardry and make Aeetes' daughter fall in love with Jason. With Medea on his side he should find it easy to carry off the golden fleece and make his way back to Iolcus. She is something of a witch herself.'

'But ladies,' said Cypris, speaking now to both of them, 'he is far more likely to obey you than me. There is no reverence in him, but faced by you he might display some spark of decent feeling. He certainly pays no attention to me: he defies me and always does the opposite of what I say. In fact I am so worn out by his naughtiness that I have half a mind to break his bow and wicked arrows in his very sight, remembering how he threatened me with them in one of his moods. He said, "If you don't keep your hands off me while I can still control my temper, you can blame yourself for the consequences."'

Hera and Athene smiled at this and exchanged glances. But Aphrodite was hurt. She said: 'Other people find my troubles amusing. I really should not speak of them to all and sundry; it is enough for me to know them. However, as you have both set your hearts on it, I will try and coax my boy. He will not refuse.'

Hera took Aphrodite's slender hand in hers and with a sweet smile replied: 'Very well, Cytherea. Play your part, just as you say; but quickly, please. And do not scold or argue with your child when he annoys you. He will improve by and by.'

With that she rose to go. Athene followed her, and the pair left for home. Cypris too set out, and after searching up and down Olympus for her boy, found him far away in the fruit-laden orchard of Zeus. With him was Ganymede, whose beauty had so captivated Zeus that he took him up to heaven to live with the immortals. The two lads, who had much in common, were playing with golden knuckle-bones. Eros, the greedy boy, was standing there with a whole handful of them clutched to his breast and a happy flush mantling his cheeks. Near by sat Ganymede, hunched up, silent and disconsolate, with only two left. He threw these for what they were worth in quick succession and was furious when Eros laughed. Of course he lost them both immediately – they joined the rest. So he went off in despair with empty hands and did not notice the goddess's approach.

Aphrodite came up to her boy, took his chin in her hand, and said: 'Why this triumphant smile, you rascal? I do believe you won the game unfairly by cheating a beginner. But listen now. Will you be good and do me a favour I am going to ask of you? Then I will give you one of Zeus's lovely toys, the one that his fond nurse Adresteia made for him in the Idaean cave when he was still a child and liked to play. It is a perfect ball; Hephaestus himself could not make you a better toy. It is made of golden hoops laced together all the way round with double stitching; but the seams are hidden by a winding, dark blue band. When you throw it up, it will leave a fiery trail behind it like a meteor in the sky. That is what I'll give you, if you let fly an arrow at Aeetes' girl and make her fall in love with Jason. But you must act at once, or I may not be so generous.'

When he heard this, Eros was delighted. He threw down all his toys, flung his arms round his mother and hung on to her skirt with both hands, imploring her to let him have the ball at once. But she gently refused, and drawing him towards her, held him close and kissed his cheeks. Then with a smile she said, 'By your own dear head and mine, I swear I will not disappoint you. You shall have the gift when you have shot an arrow into Medea's heart.'

Eros gathered up his knuckle-bones, counted them all carefully, and put them in the fold of his mother's shining robe. Fetching his quiver from where it leant against a tree, he slung it on his shoulder with a golden strap, picked up his crooked bow, and made his way through the luxuriant orchard of Zeus's palace. Then he passed through the celestial gates of Olympus, where a pathway for the gods leads down, and twin poles, earth's highest points, soar up in lofty pinnacles that catch the first rays of the risen sun. And as he swept on through the boundless air he saw an ever-changing scene beneath him, here the life-supporting land with its peopled cities and its sacred rivers, here mountain peaks, and here the all-encircling sea.

Meanwhile the Argonauts were sitting in conference on the benches of their ship where it lay hidden in the marshes of the river. Each man had taken his own seat, and Jason, who was speaking, was faced by row upon row of quiet listeners. 'My friends,' he said, 'I am going to tell you what action I myself should like to take, though its success depends on you. Sharing the danger as we do, we share the right of speech; and I warn the man who keeps his mouth shut when he ought to speak his mind that he will be the one to wreck our enterprise.

'I ask you all to stay quietly on board with your arms ready, while I go up to Aeetes' palace with the sons of Phrixus and two other men. When I see him I intend to parley with him first and find out whether he means to treat us as friends and let us have the golden fleece, or dismiss us with contempt, relying on his own power. Warned thus, by the man himself, of any evil thoughts he may be entertaining, we will decide whether to face him in the field or find some way of getting what we want without recourse to arms. We ought not to use force to rob him of his own without so much as seeing what a few words may do; it would be much better to talk to him first and try to win him over. Speech, by smoothing the way, often succeeds where forceful measures might have failed. Remember too that Aeetes welcomed the admirable Phrixus when he fled from a stepmother's treachery and a father who had planned to sacrifice him. Every man on earth, even the greatest rogue, fears Zeus the god of hospitality and keeps his laws.'

With one accord the young men approved the lord Jason's plan, and no one having risen to suggest another, he asked the sons of Phrixus, with Telamon and Augeias, to accompany him and himself took the Wand of Hermes in his hand. Leaving the ship they came to dry land beyond the reeds and water and passed on to the high ground of the plain which bears the name of Circe. Here osiers and willows stand in rows, with corpses dangling on ropes from their highest branches. To this day the Colchians would think it sacrilege to burn the bodies of their men. They never bury them or raise a mound above them, but wrap them in untanned oxhide and hang them up on trees at a distance from the town. Thus, since it is their custom to bury women, earth and air play equal parts in the disposal of their dead.

While Jason and his friends were on their way, Hera had a kindly thought for them. She covered the whole town with mist so that they might reach Aeetes' house unseen by any of the numerous Colchians. But as soon as they had come in from the country and reached the palace she dispersed the mist. At the entrance they paused for a moment to marvel at the king's courtyard with its wide gates, the rows of soaring columns round the palace walls, and high over all the marble cornice resting on triglyphs of bronze. They crossed the threshold of the court unchallenged. Near by, cultivated vines covered with greenery rose high in the air and underneath them four perennial springs gushed up. These were Hephaestus' work. One flowed with milk, and one with wine, the third with fragrant oil, while the fourth was a fountain of water which grew warm when the Pleiades set, but changed at their rising and bubbled up from the hollow rock as cold as ice. Such were the marvels that Hephaestus the great Engineer had contrived for the palace of Cytaean Aeetes. He had also made him bulls with feet of bronze and bronze mouths from which the breath came out in flame, blazing and terrible. And he had forged a plough of indurated steel, all in one piece, as a thank-offering to Helios, who had taken him up in his chariot when he sank exhausted on the battlefield of Phlegra.

There was also an inner court, with many well-made folding doors leading to various rooms, and decorated galleries to right and left. Higher buildings stood at angles to this court on either side. In one of them, the highest, King Aeetes lived with his queen; in another, his son Apsyrtus, whom a Caucasian nymph named Asterodeia had borne to him before he married Eidyia, the youngest daughter of Tethys and Ocean. 'Phaëthon' was the nickname that the young Colchians gave Apsyrtus because he outshone them all.

The other buildings housed the maidservants and Chalciope and Medea, the two daughters of Aeetes. At the moment, Medea was going from room to find her sister. The goddess Hera had kept her in the house, though as a rule she did not spend her time at home, but was busy all day in the temple of Hecate, of whom she was priestess. When she saw the men she gave a cry; Chalciope heard it, and her maids dropped their yarn and spindles on the floor and all ran out of doors.

When Chalciope saw her sons among the strangers, she lifted up her hands for joy. They greeted her in the same fashion and then in their happiness embraced her. But she had her moan to make. 'So after all,' she said, 'you were not allowed to roam so very far from your neglected mother: Fate turned you back. But how I have suffered! This mad desire of yours for Hellas! This blind obedience to your dying father's wishes! What misery, what heartache, they brought me! Why should you go to the city of Orchomenus, whoever he may be, abandoning your widowed mother for the sake of your grandfather's estate?'

Last of all, Aeetes with his queen, Eidyia, who had heard Chalciope speaking, came out of the house. And at once the whole courtyard was astir. A number of his men busied themselves over the carcass of a large bull; others chopped firewood; others heated water for the baths. Not one of them took a rest: they were working for the king.

Meanwhile Eros, passing through the clear air, had arrived unseen and bent on mischief, like a gadfly setting out to plague the grazing heifers, the fly that cowherds call the breese. In the porch, under the lintel of the door, he quickly strung his bow and from his quiver took a new arrow, fraught with pain. Still unobserved, he ran across the threshold glancing around him sharply. Then he crouched low at Jason's feet, fitted the notch to the middle of the string, and drawing the bow as far as his hands would stretch, shot at Medea. And her heart stood still.

With a happy laugh Eros sped out of the high-roofed hall on his way back, leaving his shaft deep in the girl's breast, hot as fire. Time and again she darted a bright glance at Jason. All else was forgotten. Her heart, brimful of this new agony, throbbed within her and overflowed with the sweetness of the pain.

A working woman, rising before dawn to spin and needing light in her cottage room, piles brushwood on a smouldering log, and the whole heap kindled by the little brand goes up in a mighty blaze. Such was the fire of Love, stealthy but all-consuming, that swept through Medea's heart. In the turmoil of her soul, her soft cheeks turned from rose to white and white to rose.

By now the servants had prepared a banquet for the newcomers, who gladly sat down to it after refreshing themselves in warm baths. When they had enjoyed the food and drink, Aeetes put some questions to his grandsons:

'Sons of my daughter and of Phrixus, the most deserving guest I have ever entertained, how is it that you are back in Aea? Did some misadventure cut your journey short? You refused to listen when I told you what a long way you had to go. But I knew; for I myself was whirled along it in the chariot of my father Helios, when he took my sister Circe to the Western Land and we reached the coast of Tyrrhenia, where she still lives, far, far indeed from Colchis. But enough of that. Tell me plainly what befell you, who your companions are, and where you disembarked.'

To answer these questions, Argus stepped out in front of his brothers, being the eldest of the four. His heart misgave him for Jason and his mission; but he did his best to conciliate the king. 'My lord,' he said, 'that ship of ours soon fell to pieces in a storm. We hung on to one of her planks and were cast ashore on the Island of Ares in the pitch-dark night. But Providence looked after us: there was not a sign of the War-god's birds, who used to haunt the desert isle. They were driven off by these men, who had landed on the previous day and been detained there by the will of Zeus in pity for ourselves – or was it only chance? In any case, they gave us plenty of food and clothing directly they heard the illustrious name of Phrixus, and your own, my lord, since it was your city they were bound for. As to their purpose, I will be frank with you. A certain king, wishing to banish and dispossess this man because he is the most powerful of the Aeolids, has sent him here on a desperate venture, maintaining that the House of Aeolus will not escape the inexorable wrath of Zeus, the heavy burden of their guilt, and vengeance for the sufferings of Phrixus, till the fleece returns to Hellas. The ship that brought him was built by Pallas Athene on altogether different lines from the Colchian craft, the rottenest of which, as luck would have it, fell to us. For *she* was smashed to pieces by the wind and waves, whereas the bolts of *Argo* hold her together in any gale that blows, and she runs as sweetly when the crew are tugging at the oars as she does before the wind. This ship he manned with the pick of all Achaea, and in her he has come to your city, touching at many ports and crossing formidable seas, in the hope that you will let him have the fleece. But it must be as you wish. He has not come here to force your hand. On the contrary, he is willing to repay you amply for the gift by reducing for you your bitter enemies, the Sauromatae, of whom I told him. But now you may wish to know the names and lineage of your visitors. Let me tell you. Here is the man to whom the others rallied from all parts of Hellas, Jason son of Aeson, Cretheus' son. He must be a kinsman of our own on the father's side, if he is a grandson of Cretheus, for Cretheus and Athamas were both sons of Aeolus, and our father Phrixus was a son of Athamas. Next, and in case you have heard that we have a son of Helios with us, behold the man, Augeias. And this is Telamon, son of the illustrious Aeacus, a son of Zeus himself. Much the same is true of all the rest of Jason's followers. They are all sons or grandsons of immortal gods.'

The king was filled with rage as he listened to Argus. And now, in a towering passion, he gave vent to his displeasure, the brunt of which fell on the sons of Chalciope, whom he held responsible for the presence of the rest. His eyes blazed with fury as he burst into speech:

'You scoundrels! Get out of my sight at once. Get out of my country, you and your knavish tricks, before you meet a Phrixus and a fleece you will not relish. It was no fleece that brought you and your confederates from Hellas, but a plot to seize my sceptre and my royal power. If you had not eaten at my table first, I would tear your tongues out and chop off your hands, both of them, and send you back with nothing but your feet, to teach you to think twice before starting on another expedition. As for all that about the blessed gods, it is nothing but a pack of lies.'

Telamon's gorge rose at this outburst from the angry king, and he was on the point of flinging back defiance, to his own undoing, when he was checked by Jason, who forestalled him with a more politic reply.

'My lord,' he said, 'pray overlook our show of arms. We have not come to your city and palace with any such designs as you suspect. Nor have we predatory aims. Who of his own accord would brave so vast a sea to lay his hands on other people's goods? No; it was Destiny and the cruel orders of a brutal king that sent me here. Be generous to your suppliants, and I will make all Hellas ring with the glory of your name. And by way of more immediate recompense, we are prepared to take the field in your behalf against the Sauromatae or any other tribe you may wish to subdue.'

Jason's obsequious address had no effect. The king was plunged in sullen cogitation, wondering whether to leap up and kill them on the spot or to put their powers to the proof. He ended by deciding for a test and said to Jason:

'Sir, there is no need for me to hear you out. If you are really children of the gods or have other grounds for approaching me as equals in the course of your piratical adventure, I will let you have the golden fleece – that is, if you still want it when I have put you to the proof. For I am not like your overlord in Hellas, as you describe him; I am not inclined to be ungenerous to men of rank.

'I propose to test your courage and abilities by setting you a task which, though formidable, is not beyond the strength of my two hands. Grazing on the plain of Ares, I have a pair of bronze-footed and fire-breathing bulls. These I yoke and drive over the hard fallow of the plain, quickly ploughing a four-acre field up to the ridge at either end. Then I sow the furrows, not with corn, but with the teeth of a monstrous serpent, which presently come up in the form of armed men, whom I cut down and kill with my spear as they rise up against me on all sides. It is morning when I yoke my team and by evening I have done my harvesting. That is what I do. If you, sir, can do as well, you may carry off the fleece to your king's palace on the very same day. If not, you shall not have it – do not deceive yourself. It would be wrong for a brave man to truckle to a coward.'

Jason listened to this with his eyes fixed on the floor; and when the king had finished, he sat there just as he was, without a word, resourceless in the face of his dilemma. For a long time he turned the matter over in his mind, unable boldly to accept a task so clearly fraught with peril. But at last he gave the king an answer which he thought would serve:

'Your Majesty, right is on your side and you leave me no escape whatever. Therefore I will take up your challenge, in spite of its preposterous terms, and though I may be courting death. Men serve no harsher mistress than Necessity, who drives me now and forced me to come here at another king's behest.'

He spoke in desperation and was little comforted by Aeetes' sinister reply: 'Go now and join your company: you have shown your relish for the task. But if you hesitate to yoke the bulls or shirk the deadly harvesting, I will take the matter up myself in a manner calculated to make others shrink from coming here and pestering their betters.'

He had made his meaning clear, and Jason rose from his chair. Augeias and Telamon followed him at once, and so did Argus, but without his brothers, whom he had warned by a nod to stay there for the time being. As the party went out of the hall, Jason's comeliness and charm singled him out from all the rest; and Medea, plucking her bright veil aside, turned wondering eyes upon him. Her heart smouldered with pain and as he passed from sight her soul crept out of her, as in a dream, and fluttered in his steps.

They left the palace with heavy hearts. Meanwhile Chalciope, to save herself from Aeetes' wrath, had hastily withdrawn to her own room together with her sons. Medea too retired, a prey to all the inquietude that Love awakens. The whole scene was still before her eyes – how Jason looked, the clothes he wore, the things he said, the way he sat, and how he walked to the door. It seemed to her, as she reviewed these images, that there was nobody like Jason. His voice and the honey-sweet words that he had used still rang in her ears. But she feared for him. She was afraid that the bulls or Aeetes with his own hands might kill him; and she mourned him as one already dead. The pity of it overwhelmed her; a round tear ran down her cheek; and weeping quietly she voiced her woes:

'What is the meaning of this grief? Hero or villain (and why should I care which?) the man is going to his death. Well, let him go! And yet I wish he had been spared. Yes, sovran Lady Hecate, this is my prayer. Let him live to reach his home. But if he must be conquered by the bulls, may he first learn that I for one do not rejoice in his cruel fate.'

While Medea thus tormented herself, Jason was listening to some advice from Argus, who had waited to address him till the people and the town were left behind and the party were retracing their steps across the plain.

'My lord,' he said, 'I have a plan to suggest. You will not like it; but in a crisis no expedient should be left untried. You have heard me speak of a young woman who practises witchcraft under the tutelage of the goddess Hecate. If we could win her over, we might banish from our minds all fear of your defeat in the ordeal. I am only afraid that my mother may not support me in this scheme. Nevertheless, since we all stand to lose our lives together, I will go back and sound her.'

'My friend,' said Jason, responding to the good will shown by Argus, 'if you are satisfied, then I have no objections. Go back at once and seek your mother's aid, feeling your way with care. But oh, how bleak the prospect is, with our one hope of seeing home again in women's hands!'

Soon after this they reached the marsh. Their comrades, when they saw them coming up, greeted them with cheerful enquiries, which Jason answered in a gloomy vein. 'Friends,' he said, 'if I were to answer all your questions, we should never finish; but the cruel king has definitely set his face against us. He said he had a couple of bronze-footed and fire-breathing bulls grazing on the plain of Ares, and told me to plough a four-acre field with these. He will give me seed from a serpent's jaws which will produce a crop of earthborn men in panoplies of bronze. And I have got to kill them before the day is done. That is my task. I straightway undertook it, for I had no choice.'

The task, as Jason had described it, seemed so impossible to all of them that for a while they stood there without a sound or word, looking at one another in impotent despair. But at last Peleus took heart and spoke out to his fellow chieftains: 'The time has come. We must confer and settle what to do. Not that debate will help us much: I would rather trust to strength of arm. Jason, my lord, if you fancy the adventure and mean to yoke Aeetes' bulls you will naturally keep your promise and prepare. But if you have the slightest fear that your nerve may fail you, do not force yourself. And you need not sit there looking round for someone else. I, for one, am willing. The worst that I shall suffer will be death.'

So said the son of Aeacus. Telamon too was stirred and eagerly leapt up; next Idas, full of lofty thoughts; then Castor and Polydeuces; and with them one who was already numbered with the men of might though the down was scarcely showing on his cheeks, Meleager son of Oeneus, his heart uplifted by the courage that dares all. But the others made no move, leaving it to these; and Argus addressed the six devoted men:

'My friends, you certainly provide us with a last resource. But I have some hopes of timely help that may be coming from my mother. So I advise you, keen as you are, to do as you did earlier and wait here in the ship for a little while – it is always better to think twice before one throws away one's life for nothing. There is a girl living in Aeetes' palace whom the goddess Hecate has taught to handle with extraordinary skill all the magic herbs that grow on dry land or in running water. With these she can put out a raging fire, she can stop rivers as they roar in spate, arrest a star, and check the movement of the sacred moon. We thought of her as we made our way down here from the palace. My mother, her own sister, might persuade her to be our ally in the hour of trial; and with your approval I am prepared to go back to Aeetes' palace this very day and see what I can do. Who knows? Some friendly Power may come to my assistance.'

So said Argus. And the gods were kind: they sent them a sign. In her terror, a timid dove, hotly pursued by a great hawk, dropped straight down into Jason's lap, while the hawk fell impaled on the mascot at the stern. Mopsus at once made the omens clear to all:

'It is for you, my friends, that Heaven has designed this portent. We could construe it in no better way than by approaching the girl with every plea we can devise. And I do not think she will refuse, if Phineus was right when he told us that our safety lay in Aphrodite's care; for this gentle bird whose life was spared belongs to her. May all turn out as I foresee, reading the omens with my inward eye. And so, my friends, let us invoke Cytherea's aid and put ourselves at once in the hands of Argus.'

The young men applauded, remembering what Phineus had told them. But there was one dissentient voice, and that a loud one. Idas leapt up in a towering rage and shouted: 'For shame! Have we come here to trot along with women, calling on Aphrodite to support us, instead of the mighty god of battle? Do you look to doves and hawks to get you out of trouble? Well, please yourselves! Forget that you are fighters. Pay court to girls and turn their silly heads.'

This tirade from Idas was received by many of his comrades with muttered resentment, though no one took the floor to answer him back. He sat down in high dudgeon, and Jason rose immediately to give them his decision and his orders. 'We are all agreed,' he said. 'Argus sets out from the ship. And we ourselves will now make fast with hawsers from the river to the shore, where anyone can see us. We certainly ought not to hide here any longer as though we were afraid of fighting.'

With that, he despatched Argus on his way back to the town; and the crew, taking their orders from Aeson's son, hauled the anchor-stones on board and rowed *Argo* close to dry land, a little way from the marsh.

At the same time Aeetes, meaning to play the Minyae false and do them grievous injury, summoned the Colchians to assemble, not in his palace, but at another spot where meetings had been held before. He declared that as soon as the bulls had destroyed the man who had taken up his formidable challenge, he would strip a forest hill of brushwood and burn the ship with every man on board, to cure them once and for all of the intolerable airs they gave themselves, these enterprising buccaneers. It was true that he had welcomed Phrixus to his palace, but whatever the man's plight, he certainly would not have done so, though he had never known a foreigner so gentle and so well conducted, if Zeus himself had not sent Hermes speeding down from heaven to see that he met with a sympathetic host. Much less should pirates landing in his country be left unpunished, men whose sole concern it was to get their hands on other people's goods, to lie in ambush plotting a sudden stroke, to sally out, cry havoc, and raid the farmers' yards. Moreover, Phrixus' sons should make him suitable amends for coming back in league with a gang of ruffians to hurl him from the throne. The crazy fools! But it all chimed in with an ugly hint he had had long ago from his father Helios, warning him to beware of treasonable plots and evil machinations in his own family. So, to complete their chastisement, he would pack them off to Achaea, just as they and their father had wished; and that was surely far enough. As for his daughters, he had not the slightest fear of treachery from them. Nor from his son Apsyrtus; only Chalciope's sons were involved in the mischief. The angry king ended by informing his people of the drastic measures that he had in mind, and ordering them, with many threats, to watch the ship and the men themselves so that no one should escape his doom.

By now Argus had reached the palace and was urging his mother with every argument at his command to invoke Medea's aid. The same idea had already occurred to Chalciope herself; but she had hesitated. On the one hand, she was afraid of failure: Medea might be so appalled by thoughts of her father's wrath that all entreaties would fall upon deaf ears. On the other, she feared that if her sister yielded to her prayers the whole conspiracy would be laid bare.

Meanwhile the maiden lay on her bed, fast asleep, with all her cares forgotten. But not for long. Dreams assailed her, deceitful dreams, the nightmares of a soul in pain. She dreamt that the stranger had accepted the challenge, not in the hope of winning the ram's fleece – it was not that that had brought him to Aea – but in order that he might carry her off to his own home as his bride. Then it seemed that it was she who was standing up to the bulls; she found it easy to handle them. But when all was done, her parents backed out of the bargain, pointing out that it was Jason, not their daughter, whom they had dared to yoke the bulls. This led to an interminable dispute between her father and the Argonauts, which resulted in their leaving the decision to her – she could do as she pleased. And she, without a moment's thought, turned her back on her parents and chose the stranger. Her parents were cut to the quick; they screamed in their anger; and with their cries she woke.

She sat up, shivering with fright, and peered round the walls of her bedroom. Slowly and painfully she dragged herself back to reality. Then in self-pity she cried out and voiced the terror that her nightmare had engendered:

'These noblemen, their coming here, I fear it spells catastrophe. And how I tremble for their leader! He should pay court to some Achaean girl far away in his own country, leaving me content with spinsterhood and home. Ah no! Away with modesty! I will stand aside no longer; I will go to my sister. She is anxious for her sons and well might ask me for my help in the ordeal. And so my heartache would be eased.'

With that she rose, and in her gown, with nothing on her feet, went to her bedroom door and opened it. She was resolved to go to her sister and she crossed the threshold. But once outside she stayed for a long time where she was, inhibited by shame. Then she turned and went back into the room. Again she came out of it, and again she crept back, borne to and fro on hesitating feet. Whenever she set out shame held her back; and all the time shame held her in the room shameless desire kept urging her to leave it. Three times she tried to go;

three times she failed; and at the fourth attempt she threw herself face downward on the bed and writhed in pain.

Her plight was like that of a bride mourning in her bedroom for the young husband chosen for her by her brothers and parents, and lost by some stroke of Fate before the pair had enjoyed each other's love. Too shy and circumspect as yet to mingle freely with the maids and risk an unkind word or tactless jibe, she sits disconsolate in a corner of the room, looks at the empty bed and weeps in silence though her heart is bursting. Thus Medea wept.

But presently one of the servants, her own young maid, came to the room, and seeing her mistress lying there in tears, ran off to tell Chalciope, who was sitting with her sons considering how they might win Medea over. Chalciope did not make light of the girl's story, strange as it seemed. In great alarm she hurried through the house from her own to her sister's room, and there she found her lying in misery on the bed with both cheeks torn and her eyes red with weeping.

'My dear!' she cried. 'What is the meaning of these tears? What has made you so terribly unhappy? Have you suddenly been taken ill? Or has Father told you of some awful fate he has in mind for me and my sons? Oh, how I wish I might never see this city and this home of ours again, and live at the world's end, where nobody has even heard of the Colchians!'

Medea blushed. She was eager to answer, but for a long while was checked by maiden modesty. Time and again the truth was on the tip of her tongue, only to be swallowed back. Time and again it tried to force a passage through her lovely lips, but no words came. At last, impelled by the bold hand of Love, she gave her sister a disingenuous reply: 'Chalciope, I am terrified for your sons. I am afraid that father will destroy them out of hand, strangers and all. I had a little sleep just now and in a nightmare that is what I saw. God forfend such evil! May you never have to suffer so through them!'

Medea was trying to induce her sister to make the first move and appeal to her to save her sons. And indeed Chalciope was overwhelmed by horror at her disclosure. She said: 'My fears have been the same as yours. That is what brought me here. I hoped that you and I might put our heads together and find a way of rescuing my sons. But swear by Earth and Heaven that you will keep what I say to yourself and work in league with me. I implore you, by the happy gods, by your own head, and by your parents, not to stand by while they are mercilessly done to death. If you do so, may I die with my dear sons and haunt you afterwards from Hades like an avenging Fury.'

With that she burst into tears, sank down, and throwing her arms round her sister's knees buried her head in her lap. Each of them wailed in pity for the other, and faint sounds of women weeping in distress were heard throughout the palace.

Medea was the first to speak. 'Sister,' she said, 'you left me speechless when you talked of curses and avenging Furies. How can I set your mind at rest? I only wish we could be sure of rescuing your sons. However, I will do as you ask and take the solemn oath of the Colchians, swearing by mighty Heaven and by Earth below, the

Mother of the Gods, that provided your demands are not impossible I will help you as you wish, with all the power that in me lies.'

When Medea had taken the oath, Chalciope said: 'Well now, for the sake of my sons, could you not devise some stratagem, some cunning ruse that the stranger could rely on in his trial? He needs you just as much as they do. In fact he has sent Argus here to urge me to enlist your help. I left him in the palace when I came to you just now.'

At this, Medea's heart leapt up. Her lovely cheeks were crimsoned and her eyes grew dim with tears of joy. 'Chalciope,' she cried, 'I will do anything to please you and your sons, anything to make you happy. May I never see the light of dawn again and may you see me in the world no more, if I put anything before your safety and the lives of your sons, who are my brothers, my dear kinsmen, with whom I was brought up. And you, am I not as much your daughter as your sister, you that took me to your breast as you did them, when I was a baby, as I often heard my mother say? But go now and tell no one of my promise, so that my parents may not know how I propose to keep it. And at dawn I will go to Hecate's temple with magic medicine for the bulls.'

Thus assured, Chalciope withdrew from her sister's room and brought her sons the news of her success. But Medea, left alone, fell a prey once more to shame and horror at the way in which she planned to help a man in defiance of her father's wishes.

Night threw her shadow on the world. Sailors out at sea looked up at the circling Bear and the stars of Orion.

Travellers and watchmen longed for sleep, and oblivion came at last to mothers mourning for their children's death. In the town, dogs ceased to bark and men to call to one another; silence reigned over the deepening dark. But gentle sleep did not visit Medea. In her yearning for Jason, fretful cares kept her awake. She feared the great strength of the bulls; she saw him face them in the field of Ares; she saw him meet an ignominious end. Her heart fluttered within her, restless as a patch of sunlight dancing up and down on a wall as the swirling water poured into a pail reflects it.

Tears of pity ran down her cheeks and her whole body was possessed by agony, a searing pain which shot along her nerves and deep into the nape of her neck, that vulnerable spot where the relentless archery of Love causes the keenest pangs. At one moment she thought she would give him the magic drug for the bulls; at the next she thought no, she would rather die herself; and then that she would do neither, but patiently endure her fate. In the end she sat down and debated with herself in miserable indecision:

'Evil on this side, evil on that; and must I choose between them? In either case my plight is desperate and there is no escape; this torture will go on. Oh how I wish that Artemis with her swift darts had put an end to me before I had seen that man, before Chalciope's sons had gone to Achaea! Some god, some Fury rather, must have brought them back with grief and tears for us. Let him be killed in the struggle, if it is indeed his fate to perish in the unploughed field. For how could I prepare the drug without my parents' knowledge? What story shall

I tell them? What trickery will serve? How can I help him, and fail to be found out? Are he and I to meet alone? Indeed I am ill-starred, for even if he dies I have no hope of happiness; with Jason dead, I should taste real misery. Away with modesty, farewell to my good name! Saved from all harm by me, let him go where he pleases, and let me die. On the very day of his success I could hang myself from a rafter or take a deadly poison. Yet even so my death would never save me from their wicked tongues. My fate would be the talk of every city in the world; and here the Colchian women would bandy my name about and drag it in mud – the girl who fancied a foreigner enough to die for him, disgraced her parents and her home, went off her head for love. What infamy would not be mine? Ah, how I grieve now for the folly of my passion! Better to die here in my room this very night, passing from life unnoticed, unreproached, than to carry through this horrible, this despicable scheme.'

With that she went and fetched the box in which she kept her many drugs, healing or deadly, and putting it on her knees she wept. Tears ran unchecked in torrents down her cheeks and drenched her lap as she bemoaned her own sad destiny. She was determined now to take a poison from the box and swallow it; and in a moment she was fumbling with the fastening of the lid in her unhappy eagerness to reach the fatal drug. But suddenly she was overcome by the hateful thought of death, and for a long time she stayed her hand in silent horror. Visions of life and all its fascinating cares rose up before her. She thought of the pleasures that the living can enjoy. She thought of her happy playmates, as a young girl will. And now, setting its true value on all this, it seemed to her a sweeter thing to see the sun than it had ever been before. So, prompted by Hera, she changed her mind and put the box away. Irresolute no longer, she waited eagerly for Dawn to come, so that she could meet the stranger face to face and give him the magic drug as she had promised. Time after time she opened her door to catch the first glimmer of day; and she rejoiced when early Dawn lit up the sky and people in the town began to stir.

Argus left the palace and returned to the ship. But he told his brothers to wait before following him, in order to find out what Medea meant to do. She herself, as soon she saw the first light of day, gathered up the golden locks that were floating round her shoulders in disorder, washed the stains from her cheeks and cleansed her skin with an ointment clear as nectar; then she put on a beautiful robe equipped with cunning brooches, and threw a silvery veil over her lovely head. And as she moved about, there in her own home, she walked oblivious of all evils imminent, and worse to come.

She had twelve maids, young as herself and all unmarried, who slept in the ante-chamber of her own sweet-scented room. She called them now and told them to yoke the mules to her carriage at once, as she wished to drive to the splendid Temple of Hecate; and while they were getting the carriage ready she took a magic ointment from her box. This salve was named after Prometheus. A man had only to smear it on his body, after propitiating the only-begotten Maiden with a midnight offering, to become invulnerable by sword or fire and for that day to surpass himself in strength and daring. It first appeared in a plant that sprang from the blood-like ichor of Prometheus in his torment, which the flesh-eating eagle had dropped on the spurs of Caucasus. The flowers, which grew on twin stalks a cubit high, were of the colour of Corycian saffron, while the root looked like flesh that has just been cut, and the juice like the dark sap of a mountain oak. To make the ointment, Medea, clothed in black, in the gloom of night, had drawn off this juice in a Caspian shell after bathing in seven perennial streams and calling seven times on Brimo, nurse of youth, Brimo, night-wanderer of the underworld, Queen of the dead. The dark earth shook and rumbled underneath the Titan root when it was cut, and Prometheus himself groaned in the anguish of his soul.

Such was the salve that Medea chose. Placing it in the fragrant girdle that she wore beneath her bosom, she left the house and got into her carriage, with two maids on either side. They gave her the reins, and taking the well-made whip in her right hand, she drove off through the town, while the rest of the maids tucked up their skirts above their white knees and ran behind along the broad highway, holding on to the wicker body of the carriage.

I see her there like Artemis, standing in her golden chariot after she has bathed in the gentle waters of Parthenius or the streams of Amnisus, and driving off with her fast-trotting deer over the hills and far away to some rich-scented sacrifice. Attendant nymphs have gathered at the source of Amnisus or flocked in from the glens and upland springs to follow her; and fawning beasts whimper in homage and tremble as she passes by. Thus Medea and her maids sped through the town, and on either side people made way for her, avoiding the princess's eye.

Leaving the city and its well-paved streets, she drove across the plain and drew up at the shrine. There she got quickly down from her smooth-running carriage and addressed her maids. 'My friends,' she said, 'I have done wrong. I forgot that we were told not to go among these foreigners who are wandering about the place. Everybody in the town is terrified, and in consequence none of the women who every day foregather here have come. But since we are here and it looks as though we shall be left in peace, we need not deny ourselves a little pleasure. Let us sing to our heart's content, and then, when we have gathered some of the lovely flowers in the meadow there, go back to town at the usual time. And if you will only fall in with a scheme of mine, you shall have something better than flowers to take home with you today. I will explain. Argus and Chalciope herself have persuaded me against my better judgement – but not a word to anyone of what I say; my father must not hear about it. They wish me to protect that stranger, the one who took up the challenge, in his mortal combat with the bulls and take some presents from him in return. I told them I thought well of the idea; and I have in fact invited him to come and see me here without his followers. But if he brings his gifts and hands them over, I mean to share them out among ourselves; and what we give him in return will be a deadlier drug than he expects. All I ask of you when he arrives is to leave me by myself.'

With this ingenious figment Medea satisfied her maids. Meanwhile Argus, when his brothers had told him she was going to the Temple of Hecate at dawn, drew Jason apart and conducted him across the plain. Mopsus son of Ampycus went with them, an excellent adviser for travellers setting out, and able to interpret any omen that a bird might offer on the way. As for Jason, by the grace of Hera Queen of Heaven, no hero of the past, no son of Zeus himself, no offspring of the other gods, could have outshone him on that day, he was so good to look at, so delightful to talk to. Even his companions, as they glanced at him, were fascinated by his radiant charm. For Mopsus, it was a pleasurable journey: he had a shrewd idea how it would end.

Near the shrine and beside the path they followed, there stood a poplar, flaunting its myriad leaves. It was much frequented as a roost by garrulous crows, one of which flapped its wings as they were passing by, and cawing from the tree-top expressed the sentiments of Hera:

'Who is this inglorious seer who has not had the sense to realize, what even children know, that a girl does not permit herself to say a single word of love to a young man who brings an escort with him? Off with you, foolish prophet and incompetent diviner! You certainly are not inspired by Cypris or the gentle Loves.'

Mopsus listened to the bird's remarks with a smile at the reprimand from Heaven. Turning to Jason, he said: 'Proceed, my lord, to the temple, where you will find

Medea and be graciously received, thanks to Aphrodite, who will be your ally in the hour of trial, as was foretold to us by Phineus son of Agenor. We two, Argus and I, will not go any nearer, but will wait here till you come back. You must go to her alone and attach her to yourself by your own persuasive eloquence.' This was sound advice and they both accepted it at once.

Meanwhile Medea, though she was singing and dancing with her maids, could think of one thing only. There was no melody, however gay, that did not quickly cease to please. Time and again she faltered and came to a halt. To keep her eyes fixed on her choir was more than she could do. She was for ever turning them aside to search the distant paths, and more than once she well-nigh fainted when she mistook the noise of the wind for the footfall of a passer-by.

But it was not so very long before the sight of Jason rewarded her impatient watch. Like Sirius rising from Ocean, brilliant and beautiful but full of menace for the flocks, he sprang into view, splendid to look at but fraught with trouble for the lovesick girl. Her heart stood still, a mist descended on her eyes, and a warm flush spread across her cheeks. She could neither move towards him nor retreat; her feet were rooted to the ground. And now her servants disappeared, and the pair of them stood face to face without a word or sound, like oaks or tall pines that stand in the mountains side by side in silence when the air is still, but when the wind has stirred them chatter without end. So these two, stirred by the breath of Love, were soon to pour out all their tale.

Jason, seeing how distraught Medea was, tried to put her at her ease. 'Lady,' he said, 'I am alone. Why are you so fearful of me? I am not a profligate as some men are, and never was, even in my own country. So you have no need to be on your guard, but may ask or tell me anything you wish. We have come together here as friends, in a consecrated spot which must not be profaned. Speak to me, question me, without reserve; and since you have already promised your sister to give me the talisman I need so much, pray do not put me off with pleasant speeches, I plead to you by Hecate herself, by your parents, and by Zeus. His hand protects all suppliants and strangers, and I that now address my prayers to you in my necessity am both a stranger and a suppliant. Without you and your sister I shall never succeed in my appalling task. Grant me your aid and in the days to come I will reward you duly, repaying you as best I can from the distant land where I shall sing your praises. My comrades too when they are back in Hellas will immortalize your name. So will their wives and mothers, whom I think of now as sitting by the sea, shedding tears in their anxiety for us – bitter tears, which you could wipe away. Remember Ariadne, young Ariadne, daughter of Minos and Pasiphae, who was a daughter of the Sun. She did not scruple to befriend Theseus and save him in his hour of trial; and then, when Minos had relented, she left her home and sailed away with him. She was the darling of the gods and she has her emblem in the sky: all night a ring of stars called Ariadne's Crown rolls on its way among the heavenly constellations. You too will be thanked by the gods if you save me and all my noble friends. Indeed your loveliness assures me of a kind and tender heart within.'

Jason's homage melted Medea. Turning her eyes aside she smiled divinely and then, uplifted by his praise, she looked him in the face. How to begin, she did not know; she longed so much to tell him everything at once. But with the charm, she did not hesitate; she drew it out from her sweet-scented girdle and he took it in his hands with joy. She revelled in his need of her and would have poured out all her soul to him as well, so captivating was the light of love that streamed from Jason's golden head and held her gleaming eyes. Her heart was warmed and melted like the dew on roses under the morning sun.

At one moment both of them were staring at the ground in deep embarrassment; at the next they were smiling and glancing at each other with the love-light in their eyes. But at last Medea forced herself to speak to him. 'Hear me now,' she said. 'These are my plans for you. When you have met my father and he has given you the deadly teeth from the serpent's jaws, wait for the moment of midnight and after bathing in an ever-running river, go out alone in sombre clothes and dig a round pit in the earth. There, kill a ewe and after heaping up a pyre over the pit, sacrifice it whole, with a libation of honey from the hive and prayers to Hecate, Perses' only Daughter. Then, when you have invoked the goddess duly, withdraw from the pyre. And do not be tempted to look behind you as you go, either by footfalls or the baying of hounds, or you may ruin everything and never reach your friends alive.

'In the morning, melt this charm, strip, and using

it like oil, anoint your body. It will endow you with tremendous strength and boundless confidence. You will feel yourself a match, not for mere men, but for the gods themselves. Sprinkle your spear and shield and sword with it as well; and neither the spear-points of the earth-born men nor the consuming flames that the savage bulls spew out will find you vulnerable. But you will not be immune for long – only for the day. Nevertheless, do not at any moment flinch from the encounter.

'And here is something else that will stand you in good stead. You have yoked the mighty bulls; you have ploughed the stubborn fallow (with those great hands and all that strength it will not take you long); you have sown the serpent's teeth in the dark earth; and now the giants are springing up along the furrows. Watch till you see a number of them rise from the soil, then, before they see you, throw a great boulder in among them; and they will fall on it like famished dogs and kill one another. That is your moment; plunge into the fray yourself.

'And so the task is done and you can carry off the fleece to Hellas – a long, long way from Aea, I believe. Go none the less, go where you will; go where the fancy takes you when you part from us.'

After this, Medea was silent for a while. She kept her eyes fixed on the ground, and the warm tears ran down her lovely cheeks as she saw him sailing off over the high seas far away from her. Then she looked up at him and sorrowfully spoke again, taking his right hand in hers and no longer attempting to conceal her love. She said:

'But do remember, if you ever reach your home. Remember the name of Medea, and I for my part will remember you when you are far away. But now, pray tell me where you live. Where are you bound for when you sail across the sea from here? Will your journey take you near the wealthy city of Orchomenus or the Isle of Aea? Tell me too about that girl you mentioned, who won such fame for herself, the daughter of Pasiphae my father's sister.'

As he listened to this and noted her tears, unconscionable Love stole into the heart of Jason too. He replied: 'Of one thing I am sure. If I escape and live to reach Achaea; if Aeetes does not set us a still more formidable task; never by night or day shall I forget you. But you asked about the country of my birth. If it pleases you to hear, I will describe it; indeed I should like nothing better. It is a land ringed by lofty mountains, rich in sheep and pasture, and the birthplace of Prometheus' son, the good Deucalion, who was the first man to found cities, build temples to the gods and rule mankind as king. Its neighbours call the land Haemonia, and in it stands Iolcus, my own town, and many others too where the very name of the Aeaean Island is unknown. Yet they do say that it was from these parts that the Aeolid Minyas migrated long ago to found Orchomenus, which borders on Cadmeian lands. But why do I trouble you with all this tiresome talk about my home and Minos' daughter, the far-famed Ariadne, that lovely lady with the glorious name who roused your curiosity? I can only hope that, as Minos came to terms with Theseus for her sake, your father will be reconciled with us.'

He had thought, by talking in this gentle way, to soothe Medea. But she was now obsessed by the gloomiest forebodings; embittered too. And she answered him with passion:

'No doubt in Hellas people think it right to honour their agreements. But Aeetes is not the kind of man that Minos was, if what you say of him is true; and as for Ariadne, I cannot claim to be a match for her. So do not talk of friendliness to strangers. But oh, at least remember me when you are back in Iolcus; and I, despite my parents, will remember you. And may there come to me some whisper from afar, some bird to tell the tale, when you forget me. Or may the Storm-Winds snatch me up and carry me across the sea to Iolcus, to denounce you to your face and remind you that I saved your life. That is the moment I would choose to pay an unexpected visit to your house.'

As she spoke, tears of misery ran down her cheeks. But Jason said: 'Dear lady, you may spare the wandering Winds that task, and your tell-tale bird as well, for you are talking nonsense. If you come to us in Hellas you will be honoured and revered by both the women and the men. Indeed they will treat you as a goddess, because it was through you that their sons came home alive, or their brothers, kinsmen, or beloved husbands were saved from hurt. And there shall be a bridal bed for you, which you and I will share. Nothing shall part us in our love till Death at his appointed hour removes us from the light of day.'

As she heard these words of his, her heart melted within her. And yet she shuddered as she thought of the disastrous step she was about to take. Poor girl! She was not going to refuse for long this offer of a home in Hellas.

The goddess Hera had arranged it all; Medea was to leave her native land for the sacred city of Iolcus, and there to bring his punishment to Pelias.

Her maids, who had been spying on them from afar, were now becoming restive, though they did not intervene. It was high time for the maiden to go home to her mother. But Medea had no thought of leaving yet; she was entranced both by his comeliness and his bewitching talk. At last however, Jason, who had kept his wits about him, said, 'Now we must part, or the sun will set before we know it. Besides, some passer-by might see us. But we will meet each other here again.'

By gentle steps they had advanced so far towards an understanding. And now they parted, he in a joyful mood to go back to his companions and the ship, she to rejoin her maids, who all ran up to meet her. But as they gathered round, she did not even notice them: her head was in the clouds. Without knowing what she did, she got into her carriage to drive the mules, taking the reins in one hand and the whip in the other. And off they trotted to the palace in the town.

She had no sooner arrived than Chalciope questioned her anxiously about her sons. But Medea had left her wits behind her. She neither heard a word her sister said nor showed the least desire to answer her inquiries. She sat down on a low stool at the foot of her bed, leant over and rested her cheek on her left hand, pondering with tears in her eyes on the infamous part she had played in a scene that she herself had staged.

Jason found his escort in the place where he had left them, and as they set out to rejoin the rest, he told them how he had fared. When the party reached the ship, he was received with open arms and in reply to the questions of his friends he told them of Medea's plans and showed them the powerful charm. Idas was the only member of the company who was not impressed. He sat aloof, nursing his resentment. The rest were overjoyed, and since the night permitted no immediate move, they settled down in peace and comfort. But at dawn they despatched two men to Aeetes to ask him for the seed, Telamon beloved of Ares, and Aethalides the famous son of Hermes. This pair set out on their errand, and they did not fail. When they reached the king, he handed them the deadly teeth that Jason was to sow.

The teeth were those of the Aonian serpent, the guardian of Ares' spring, which Cadmus killed in Ogygian Thebes. He had come there in his search for Europa, and there he settled, under the guidance of a heifer picked out for him by Apollo in an oracle. Athene, Lady of Trito, tore the teeth out of the serpent's jaws and divided them between Aeetes and Cadmus, the slayer of the beast. Cadmus sowed them in the Aonian plain and founded an earthborn clan with all that had escaped the spear of Ares when he did his harvesting. Such were the teeth that Aeetes let them take back to the ship. He gave them willingly, as he was satisfied that Jason, even if he yoked the bulls, would prove unable to finish off the task.

It was evening. Out in the west, beyond the farthest Ethiopian hills, the Sun was sinking under the darkening world; Night was harnessing her team; and the Argonauts were preparing their beds by the hawsers of the ship. But Jason waited for the bright constellation of the

Bear to decline, and then, when all the air from heaven to earth was still, he set out like a stealthy thief across the solitary plain. During the day he had prepared himself, and so had everything he needed with him; Argus had fetched him some milk and a ewe from a farm; the rest he had taken from the ship itself. When he had found an unfrequented spot in a clear meadow under the open sky, he began by bathing his naked body reverently in the sacred river, and then put on a dark mantle which Hypsipyle of Lemnos had given him to remind him of their passionate embraces. Then he dug a pit a cubit deep, piled up billets, and laid the sheep on top of them after cutting its throat. He kindled the wood from underneath and poured mingled libations on the sacrifice, calling on Hecate Brimo to help him in the coming test. This done, he withdrew; and the dread goddess, hearing his words from the abyss, came up to accept the offering of Aeson's son. She was garlanded by fearsome snakes that coiled themselves round twigs of oak; the twinkle of a thousand torches lit the scene; and hounds of the underworld barked shrilly all around her. The whole meadow trembled under her feet, and the nymphs of marsh and river who haunt the fens by Amarantian Phasis cried out in fear. Jason was terrified; but even so, as he retreated, he did not once turn round. And so he found himself among his friends once more, and Dawn arrived, showing herself betimes above the snows of Caucasus.

At daybreak too, Aeetes put on his breast the stiff cuirass which Ares had given him after slaying Mimas with his own hands in the field of Phlegra; and on his head he set his golden helmet with its four plates, bright as the Sun's round face when he rises fresh from Ocean Stream. And he took up his shield of many hides, and his unconquerable spear, a spear that none of the Argonauts could have withstood, now that they had deserted Heracles, who alone could have dealt with it in battle. Phaëthon was close at hand, holding his father's swift horses and well-built chariot in readiness. Aeetes mounted, took the reins in his hands, and drove out of the town along the broad highway to attend the contest, followed by hurrying crowds. Lord of the Colchians, he might have been Poseidon in his chariot driving to the Isthmian Games, to Taenarum, to the waters of Lerna, or through the grove of Onchestus, and on to Calaurea with his steeds, to the Haemonian Rock or the woods of Geraestus.

Meanwhile Jason, remembering Medea's instructions, melted the magic drug and sprinkled his shield with it and his sturdy spear and sword. His comrades watched him and put his weapons to the proof with all the force they had. But they could not bend the spear at all; even in their strong hands it proved itself unbreakable. Idas was furious with them. He hacked at the butt-end of the spear with his great sword, but the blade rebounded from it like a hammer from the anvil. And a great shout of joy went up; they felt that the battle was already won.

Next, Jason sprinkled his own body and was imbued with miraculous, indomitable might. As his hands increased in power, his very fingers twitched. Like a warhorse eager for battle, pawing the ground, neighing, pricking its ears and tossing up its head in pride, he exulted in the strength of his limbs. Time and again he leapt high in the air this way and that, brandishing his shield of bronze and ashen spear. The weapons flashed on the eye like intermittent lightning playing in a stormy sky from black clouds charged with rain.

After that there was no faltering; the Argonauts were ready for the test. They took their places on the benches of the ship and rowed her swiftly upstream to the plain of Ares. This lay as far beyond the city as a chariot has to travel from start to turning-post when the kinsmen of a dead king are holding foot and chariot races in his honour. They found Aeetes there and a full gathering of the Colchians. The tribesmen were stationed on the rocky spurs of Caucasus, and the king was wheeling around in his chariot on the river-bank.

Jason, as soon as his men had made the hawsers fast, leapt from the ship and entered the lists with spear and shield. He also took with him a shining bronze helmet full of sharp teeth, and his sword was slung from his shoulder. But his body was bare, so that he looked like Apollo of the golden sword as much as Ares god of war. Glancing round the field, he saw the bronze yoke for the bulls and beside it the plough of indurated steel, all in one piece. He went up to them, planted his heavy spear in the ground by its butt and laid the helmet down, leaning it against the spear. Then he went forward with his shield alone to examine the countless tracks that the bulls had made. And now, from somewhere in the bowels of the earth, from the smoky stronghold where they slept, the pair of bulls appeared, breathing flames of fire. The Argonauts were terrified at the sight. But Jason planting his feet apart stood to receive them, as a reef in the sea confronts the tossing billows in a gale. He held his shield in front of him, and the two bulls, bellowing loudly, charged and butted it with their strong horns. But he was not shifted from his stance, not by so much as an inch. The bulls snorted and spurted from their mouths devouring flames, like a perforated crucible when the leather bellows of the smith, sometimes ceasing, sometimes blowing hard, have made a blaze and the fire leaps up from below with a terrific roar. The deadly heat assailed him on all sides with the force of lightning. But he was protected by Medea's magic. Seizing the right-hand bull by the tip of its horn, he dragged it with all his might towards the yoke, and then brought it down on its knees with a sudden kick on its bronze foot. The other charged, and was felled in the same way at a single blow; and Jason, who had cast his shield aside, stood with his feet apart, and though the flames at once enveloped him, held them both down on their fore-knees where they fell. Aeetes marvelled at the man's strength.

Castor and Polydeuces picked up the yoke and gave it to Jason – they had been detailed for the task and were close at hand. Jason bound it tight on the bulls' necks, lifted the bronze pole between them and fastened it to the yoke by its pointed end, while the Twins backed out of the heat and returned to the ship. Then, taking his shield from the ground he slung it on his back, picked up the heavy helmet full of teeth and grasped his unconquerable spear, with which, like some ploughman using his Pelasgian goad, he pricked the bulls under their flanks and with a firm grip on its well-made handle guided the adamantine plough.

At first the bulls in their high fury spurted flames of fire. Their breath came out with a roar like that of the blustering wind that causes frightened mariners to take in sail. But presently, admonished by the spear, they went ahead, and the rough fallow cleft by their own and the great ploughman's might lay broken up behind them. The huge clods as they were torn away along the furrow groaned aloud; and Jason came behind, planting his feet down firmly on the field. As he ploughed he sowed the teeth, casting them far from himself with many a backward glance lest a deadly crop of earthborn men should catch him unawares. And the bulls, thrusting their bronze hoofs into the earth, toiled on till only a third of the passing day was left. Then, when weary labourers in other fields were hoping it would soon be time to free their oxen from the yoke, this indefatigable ploughman's work was done – the whole four-acre field was ploughed.

Jason freed his bulls from the plough and shooed them off. They fled across the plain; and he, seeing that no earthborn men had yet appeared in the furrows, seized the occasion to go back to the ship, where his comrades gathered round him with heartening words. He dipped his helmet in the flowing river and with its water quenched his thirst, then flexed his knees to keep them supple; and as fresh courage filled his heart, he lashed himself into a fury, like a wild boar when it whets its teeth to face the hunt and the foam drips to the ground from its savage mouth.

By now the earthborn men were shooting up like corn in all parts of the field. The deadly War-god's sacred plot bristled with stout shields, double-pointed spears, and glittering helmets. The splendour of it flashed through the air above and struck Olympus. Indeed this army springing from the earth shone out like the full congregation of the stars piercing the darkness of a murky night, when snow lies deep and the winds have chased the wintry clouds away. But Jason did not forget the counsel he had had from Medea of the many wiles. He picked up from the field a huge round boulder, a formidable quoit that Ares might have thrown, but four strong men together could not have budged from its place. Rushing forward with this in his hands he hurled it far away among the earthborn men, then crouched behind his shield, unseen and full of confidence. The Colchians gave a mighty shout like the roar of the sea beating on jagged rocks; and the king himself was astounded as he saw the great quoit hurtle through the air. But the earthborn men, like nimble hounds, leapt on one another and with loud yells began to slay. Beneath each other's spears they fell on their mother earth, as pines or oaks are blown down by a gale. And now, like a bright meteor that leaps from heaven and leaves a fiery trail behind it, portentous to all those who see it flash across the night, the son of Aeson hurled himself on them with his sword unsheathed and in promiscuous slaughter mowed them down, striking as he could, for many of them had but half emerged and showed their flanks and bellies only, some had their shoulders clear, some had just stood up, and others were afoot already and rushing into battle. So might some farmer threatened by a frontier war snatch up a newly sharpened sickle and, lest the enemy should reap his fields before him, hasten to cut down the unripe corn, not waiting for the season and the sun to ripen it. Thus Jason cut his crop of earthborn men. Blood filled the furrows as water fills the conduits of a spring. And still they fell, some on their faces biting the rough clods, some on their backs, and others on their hands and sides, looking like monsters from the sea. Many were struck before they could lift up their feet, and rested there with the death-dew on their brows, each trailing on the earth so much of him as had come up into the light of day. They lay like saplings in an orchard bowed to the ground when Zeus has sent torrential rain and snapped them at the root, wasting the gardeners' toil and bringing heartbreak to the owner of the plot, the man who planted them.

Such was the scene that King Aeetes now surveyed, and such his bitterness. He went back to the city with his Colchians, pondering on the quickest way to bring the foreigners to book. And the sun sank and Jason's task was done.

Glossary

The names of only the more important characters, human and divine, are included. The geographical entries (also limited in number) are designed as a help to those who wish to follow the voyages of *Argo* with the aid of a modern atlas.

ACHERUSIAS. A promontory on the Bithynian coast near the ancient town of Heracleia; the modern Cape Baba.

AEA. The capital city of Colchis and home of King Aeetes. The name Aea or Aeaea was also given to the home of Circe, sister of Aeetes, on the west coast of Italy.

AEĒTĒS. Son of Helios the Sun and Perse; king of the Colchians; brother of Circe; father of Apsyrtus, Chalciope, and Medea.

AEOLUS. Son of Hellen; father of Athamas; grandfather of Phrixus. His sons and descendants were called Aeolids.

AESON. Father of Jason; excluded from the throne of Iolcus by his half-brother Pelias, but allowed (according to Apollonius) to remain in the city.

AETHALIDĒS. Son of Hermes and Eupolemeia; the herald of the Argonauts.

AMYCUS. King of the Bebryces, a tribe whom the Argonauts encounter on the Bithynian coast.

ANAŪRUS. A river of Thessaly flowing into the Gulf of Pagasae.

ANCĀEUS. Son of Lycurgus of Tegea; the Argonaut who is allotted the seat in *Argo* next to Heracles.

ANCĀEUS. Son of Poseidon and Astypalae; the Argonaut who takes the helm after the death of Tiphys.

APHRODĪTĒ. Daughter of Zeus; goddess of love; wife of Hephaestus; mother of Eros; also called Cytherea, Cypris, and Queen of Eryx in Sicily.

APOLLO. Son of Zeus and Leto; god of prophecy, of the arts, of healing, and of embarkation and happy landings; also called Phoebus and Phoebus Apollo.

APSYRTUS. Son of Aeetes and Asterodeia; half-brother of Medea; also called Phaëthon, the Shining One.

ARĒS. Son of Zeus and Hera; god of war.

ARĒTĒ. Wife of Alcinous the Phaeacian king.

ARGUS. Son of Arestor; the builder of *Argo*; does not figure in the tale after his namesake has appeared on the scene.

ARGUS. Son of Phrixus and Chalciope. *See under* PHRIXUS.

ARIADNĒ. Daughter of Minos and Pasiphae. *See under* THESEUS.

ARTEMIS. Daughter of Zeus and Leto; goddess of the chase and protectress of wild animals. It was one of her functions to kill women with her darts, i.e. she administered sudden death by disease.

ASSYRIA. A district of Asia Minor lying on the north coast in the neighbourhood of the Rivers Halys and

Iris. It was inhabited by the Leucosyri or White Syrians.

ATHAMAS. Father of Helle and Phrixus (*q.v.*); king of Orchomenus.

ATHĒNĒ. Daughter of Zeus; goddess of wisdom and patroness of the arts and crafts; also called Pallas Athene, and the Lady of Trito in reference to her birth, from the head of Zeus, at the Tritonian lagoon in Libya.

AUGEĪAS. Son of Helios (?); the Argonaut who is introduced to King Aeetes as his half-brother but not recognized by him as such.

BITHYNIA. A district of Asia Minor lying on the north coast, and bounded on the west by Mysia, on the east by Paphlagonia.

BORĔAS. The North Wind; father of Zetes and Calaïs and of Cleopatra wife of Phineus.

BRĬMO. A somewhat obscure goddess of the underworld whom Apollonius identifies with Hecate.

CALAÏS. Son of Boreas and Oreithyia; brother of Zetes.

CANTHUS. Son of Canethus; an Argonaut who is killed in Libya.

CARAMBIS. A promontory on the Paphlagonian coast; the modern Cape Kerempeh.

CASTOR. Son of Tyndareus (or Zeus?) and Lede; twin brother of Polydeuces (*q.v.*).

CHALCIŎPĒ. Daughter of King Aeetes and Eidyia; elder sister of Medea; widow of Phrixus; mother of Argus and his three brothers.

CHEĪRON. Son of Cronos and Philyra; the Centaur who looked after Achilles and Aristaeus in their infancy.

CIRCĒ. Daughter of Helios the Sun and Perse; sister of Aeetes; aunt of Medea.

COLCHIS. A land lying at the eastern end of the Black Sea and including part of the Caucasus; the kingdom of Aeetes; also called Cytaïs.

CRONOS. Son of Uranus and Earth; father, by Rhea, of Zeus, Poseidon, Hades, Hera and Demeter; the ex-King of Heaven who was deposed by Zeus.

CYANEAN ROCKS. The legendary Symplegades or Clashing Rocks, situated at the northern end of the Bosporus.

CYPRIS. *See under* APHRODITE.

CYTHERĒA. *See under* APHRODITE.

CYZICUS. King of the Doliones. The city of Cyzicus stood on an island close to the southern or Phrygian shore of the Propontis. Here was Mt Dindymum or Bear Mountain, one of the seats of the goddess Rhea (*q.v.*), the 'Dindymian Mother'.

DINDYMUM. *See under* CYZICUS.

DIONȲSUS. Son of Zeus and Semele; god of the vine; worshipped with orgiastic rites.

EĪDȲIA. Daughter of Tethys and Ocean; consort of King Aeetes, and mother of Chalciope and Medea.

ĔRĂTŌ. The Muse of love-songs and wedding festivities.

EROS. Son of Aphrodite; the little god of love; known to the Romans as Cupido, and sometimes multiplied.

EUPHĒMUS. Son of Poseidon and Europa; a leading Argonaut.

GLAUCUS. A minor marine divinity.

HĀDĒS. Son of Cronos and Rhea; god of the dead, who received the underworld as his portion when he and his brothers Zeus and Poseidon divided the world between them. Apollonius also uses Hades as a place name, just as we do.

HAĒMONIA. An ancient name of Thessaly in northern Greece.

HALYS. A river of Asia Minor flowing into the Black Sea east of Sinope; the modern Kizil Irmak.

HECĂTĒ. Daughter of Perses and Asteria; a goddess of the underworld and of witchcraft who is not mentioned by Homer. When Apollonius writes of 'the only-begotten Maiden' he means Hecate, not Persephone daughter of Demeter.

HĒLIOS. The Sun-god; father, by Perse, of Aeetes, Circe, and Pasiphae; and, by Clymene, of Phaëthon; also of Augeias (*q.v.*).

HĒPHAĒSTUS. Son of Zeus and Hera; husband of Aphrodite; the lame Master-Smith and Artificer of Olympus.

HĒRACLĒS. Son of Zeus and Alcmene; hero of the Twelve Labours.

HĒRA. Daughter of Cronos and Rhea; sister and wife of Zeus; queen of Olympus.

HERMĒS. Son of Zeus and Maia; ambassador of the Olympians; god of dreams.
Book IV, 522–7 is one of those passages which suggest that Apollonius abridged the first version of his poem. In our version there is no mention of a previous visit of Jason's to the Hylleans.

HYPSĬPȲLĒ. Daughter of Thoas king of Lemnos.

IDAS. Son of Aphareus; a quarrelsome and insubordinate Argonaut.

IDMON. Son of Abas (or Apollo?); a seer who sailed in *Argo* but perished in Bithynia.

IOLCUS. A town in Thessaly not far from the northern shore of the Gulf of Pagasae; the capital city of Pelias' kingdom and the home town of Jason. Recent excavations show that it was an important city as far back as the fifteenth century B.C.

IRIS. A messenger of the Olympian gods.

IRIS. A river of Asia Minor flowing into the Black Sea east of the River Halys; the modern Yeshil Irmak.

JASON. Son of Alcimede and Aeson the rightful king of Iolcus; leader of the Argonautic expedition.

LEMNOS. A large island in the northern part of the Aegean Sea.

LĒTŌ. Mother, by Zeus, of Apollo and Artemis.

LȲCUS. Son of Dascylus; king of the Mariandyni, a people visited by the Argonauts on the Bithynian coast.

MĒDĒA. Daughter of King Aeetes and Eidyia; sister of Chalciope.

MELEĀGER. Son of Oeneus and Althaea. In his youth, sails in *Argo*. His later exploits are described by Homer (*Iliad* IX).

MINYAE. A Greek race whose ancestral hero was Minyas. Apollonius uses the name for the Argonauts in general.

MOPSUS. Son of Ampycus; soothsayer of the Argonauts up to the time of his death in Libya.

MYSIA. A district of Asia Minor lying on the south coast of the Propontis.

ORCHOMENUS. Son of Minyas; king of the Minyan city of Orchomenus in Boeotia.

PAPHLAGONIA. A district of northern Asia Minor extending from Bithynia on the west to the River Halys on the east.

PELASGIAN. A name given by the Greeks to their country and its earliest inhabitants.

PĒLĒUS. Son of Aeacus; husband of Thetis; father of Achilles; one of the leading Argonauts.

PĔLIAS. Son of Poseidon and Tyro; the unrightful king of Iolcus who sent Jason out in quest of the golden fleece; father of Acastus, an Argonaut.

PERSĔPHŎNĒ. Daughter of Demeter; wife of Hades; queen of the dead.

PHAËTHON. Nickname of King Aeetes' son Apsyrtus (*q.v.*).

PHĀSIS. A river flowing through Colchis and debouching into the eastern part of the Black Sea.

PHĪNEŪS. Son of Agenor; husband of Cleopatra (daughter of Boreas and sister of Zetes and Calaïs); a blind prophet visited by the Argonauts in his home on the coast of Thynia (*q.v.*).

PHOEBUS. *See under* APOLLO.

PHRIXUS. Phrixus and Helle were children of Athamas (son of Aeolus and king of Orchomenus) by his first wife Nephele. Ino, the second wife of Athamas, was jealous of her step-children. Distorting an oracle concerning a pest that was afflicting the country, she suggested to Athamas that Phrixus should be sacrificed. Phrixus escaped, together with Helle, on the back of a flying ram with a golden fleece provided for them by the god Hermes. Helle fell off the ram's back and was drowned in the Hellespont (Dardanelles). But the golden ram encouraged Phrixus to proceed and eventually landed him in Colchis, where it was sacrificed to Zeus. Phrixus gave its fleece to Aeetes, king of Colchis, and in return the king gave him his daughter Chalciope in marriage. They had four sons, Argus, Cytissorus, Melas and Phrontis. On his deathbed, Phrixus told these sons of his to travel to Orchomenus in the hope of recovering the estate of their grandfather Athamas, who, in the interval, had been banished from his kingdom. On their way they were shipwrecked and picked up by Jason, as Apollonius relates in Book II.

PHRYGIA. *See under* CYZICUS.

POLYDĒUCĒS. Son of Lede and Tyndareus (or Zeus? Apollonius impartially calls him son of Tyndareus and son of Zeus); the patron of boxers, known also as Pollux. He and his twin brother Castor were worshipped as the protectors of travellers by sea.

POSEIDON. Son of Cronos and Rhea; younger brother of Zeus; chief god of the sea and also god of horses; husband of Amphitrite.

PROMĒTHEŪS. Son of the Titan Iapetus; punished by Zeus for having given fire to man.

RHĔA. Wife of Cronos; Mother of the chief gods of the last Olympian régime. She was identified with a Phrygian nature-goddess 'the Great Mother', and called Cybele and Dindymene. *See also under* CYZICUS.

SINŌPĒ. The name of this ingenious virgin was given to the city of Sinope (a colony of Miletus) on the Paphlagonian coast, west of the mouth of the River Halys; modern name, Sinub.

TELAMON. Son of Aeacus; father of Aias; one of the leading Argonauts.

THĒBES. The chief city of Boeotia in Greece.

THĔMIS. Daughter of Uranus and Earth; divine exponent of law and order.

THERMODON. A small river flowing into the Black Sea, east of the River Iris, near Themiscyra; the modern Termeh.

THĒSEUS. Son of Aegeus king of Athens; failed to join the Argonauts, but is mentioned as the hero who slew the Minotaur in the Cretan labyrinth with the help of Ariadne daughter of Minos, and later deserted her in the Isle of Dia or Naxos.

THŸNIA. There is some doubt concerning the location of this land where Phineus lived, but Apollonius clearly places Phineus' home on the west or European coast of the Bosporus, facing Bithynia on the east, and some way south of the Clashing Rocks.

TIPHYS. Son of Hagnias; steersman of *Argo* till his death in Bithynia.

TYNDARĔUS. Husband of Lede. *See under* POLYDEUCES.

TYRRHĒNIA. The Greek name for Etruria or Tuscany. The Etruscans are thought to have come to Italy from Asia Minor, a view which Apollonius seems to endorse by recording their occupation of Lemnos.

URĂNUS. Husband of Earth, and Father of Cronos, who

supplanted him in Olympus, only to be supplanted himself by Zeus.

ZĒTĒS. Brother of Calaïs (*q.v.*).

ZEUS. Son of Cronos and Rhea; the supreme Olympian god. Apollonius makes several references to his infancy, which was spent in a cavern on Mt Dicte in Crete.